phy Wife

Trophy Wife

Trophy Wife

Ashley & JaQuavis

www.urbanbooks.net

Urban Books, LLC
97 N18th Street
Wyandanch, NY 11798

ISBN 13: 978-1-60162-593-9
ISBN 10: 1-60162-593-6

First Mass Market Printing July 2010
First Trade Paperback Printing October 2008
Printed in the United States of America

10 9 8 7 6 5

Distributed by Kensington Publishing Corp.
Submit Wholesale Orders to:
Kensington Publishing Corp.
C/O Penguin Group (USA) Inc.
Attention: Order Processing
405 Murray Hill Parkway
East Rutherford, NJ 07073-2316
Phone: 1-800-526-0275
Fax: 1-800-227-9604

Prologue

Harlem Book Fair 2006

"Yo, it's hotter than a mu'fucka out here," JaQuavis complained as he took off his NY fitted cap and fanned himself.

"Hell, yeah. I'm 'bout to sweat out my wrap." Ashley let out a slight giggle.

The authors were sitting under a tent signing a book for one of their loyal fans. It was the biggest and most important book event of the year. Everyone who was anyone in the street-fiction game was there. It was an opportunity for the authors and readers to interact and discuss African American literature. After signing their novel, they both thanked the reader and scanned the block, which was full of excitement and chatter. It was ninety-five-degree weather and a clear, bright day in Harlem, New York as African Americans pulled together to enjoy the literary experience. And nothing but beautiful black people filled the historic streets in a scene reminiscent of the Harlem Renaissance.

JaQuavis lifted his shirt slightly to let some cool air get under his tee.

Ashley noticed his black .45 tucked in his waist. "Boy, put yo' damn shirt down. I don't know why you always bring that thing with you." She shook her head from side to side and rolled her eyes under her oversized Christian Dior shades. She hated when he toted his pistol in places where it wasn't needed.

On the other hand she knew why he toted it. He would always say, "Niggas won't catch me slipping in New Yiddy."

They knew when cats were out of town, their chances of getting caught slipping by stickup kids were very high. They would never get caught in that situation.

"Oh! I forgot," he said, quickly dropping his shirt over his weapon. He quickly sat down and began to look around for something.

Ashley followed suit and sat down. She knew exactly what he was searching for. She pulled her extra-large Gucci purse from under the table and opened it up discreetly so he could drop his gun inside.

"Good looking out," JaQuavis said as he relieved himself of a felony waiting to happen.

Just as he dropped the gun inside, Ashley noticed something funny.

"Yo, Qua, why the fuck is that nigga grilling us like that?" She discreetly glanced across the street at a young man with a NY hat on that covered his eyes.

JaQuavis instantly looked over at the dude, and Ashley's suspicions were on point. The man was definitely staring a hole through them. His hand tucked in his waist, he just stood there sticking out like a sore thumb. While everyone else at the fair was conversing and walking, he stood in the middle of the madness, ice-grilling.

JaQuavis looked back to make sure the guy was looking at them. "Yo, I don't know, but the nigga is definitely staring." Once he saw that there was no one behind him, he got on his shit.

"Yo, pass me that thing," he whispered to Ashley as he slowly sat down.

Before Ashley could even respond, the guy was coming toward them both. He had his hands tucked in his shirt and kept glancing around to see if anyone was looking. As he reached the table he was pulling something out of his pants. The two authors couldn't even react quickly enough.

Boom! The thud of a bulky white envelope hit the table.

Ashley and JaQuavis stared at the envelope, hearts racing, thinking that something was about to pop off.

The young thug calmly looked at both of them. "Yo, are you guys Ashley and JaQuavis?"

"Yeah, that's us," Ashley said with a confident smile, pretending that he didn't scare the living shit out of her.

"That is from my man Kalil. He is locked up upstate and really wants to talk to the two of you." The guy's piercing eyes shifted back and forth at both of them.

"What do you mean?" JaQuavis looked at the man suspiciously.

The man noticed JaQuavis's uneasiness and quickly made it known that it was all love. "Nah, nah. It ain't like that, fam. Look in the envelope," the man said as he gently pushed it toward him.

Ashley picked up the envelope, while JaQuavis kept his eyes on the man.

"Yo, Qua, look at this shit," Ashley said as she thumbed through the hundred-dollar bills in the envelope.

JaQuavis glanced over at the cash, and it immediately gained all of his attention. "What's this for?" He looked back at the man.

"Just to talk. Kalil really wants to speak with you personally. He told me to give both of you some incentive, nah mean?"

"So, he gave us this . . . just to talk to us." Ashley knew that there had to be a catch, because ain't shit in this world free.

"Yep! That's it. No strings attached, ma. His next visiting day is on Monday." The man pulled out a small piece of paper with Kalil's prison number and visiting hours written on it. With that he walked away, leaving both of the authors with nearly $10,000.

JaQuavis looked over at Ashley. "What the fuck was that?"

"I don't know, but I'm about to bounce before he comes back. I'm going shopping, my nigga!" Ashley smiled and stood up.

JaQuavis laughed lightly and scooped up the paper with the information on it.

"Why would he want to talk to us?" Ashley asked as they walked the corridors of the prison to see the man who'd left them all the cash.

The situation had piqued their interest, and they were too curious not to follow through with the visit. After much thought, they both agreed and decided to give the man a visit. They figured, if he was willing to pay ten stacks for a conversation, then he must've had something important to talk about.

"I don't know. We about to find out, though," JaQuavis answered as they went through the irritating search.

After a twenty-minute process, they entered the waiting room and walked over to the sign-in desk. JaQuavis took his finger and scrolled down to see what booth Kalil Kelly was in.

"Table seventeen," he said.

They both headed toward the booth, where a man in an orange jumpsuit was patiently waiting at the steel table. He looked to be in his late twenties or early thirties and was average sized. He had his hands folded, handcuffs dangling off his wrists.

JaQuavis was the first to take a seat in front of the man, and Ashley followed close behind. Ashley examined the man's eyes and a look of sincerity was embedded within his pupils. In a brief moment of silence, the man looked into both of the authors' faces with his brown eyes, the bags underneath his eyes displaying his stressful times and hardship.

"Hello. I'm Kalil," the man said in a strong New York accent.

JaQuavis calmly nodded his head. Ashley remained silent as she sized up Kalil, searching for his hidden agenda.

"Thanks for coming to see me. I know this is odd. I sent my old cellmate to reach you both at the book fair because I really need to talk to the two of you."

"We got your package. We don't feel that it is necessary. We know nothing in this world is free." Ashley crossed her hands and stared at the man across from her.

"Yeah, we can't accept that, fam. You can tell your people that they can come and pick it up." JaQuavis leaned back in his chair. "What is it exactly that you wanted to speak with us about? I mean, it must be important. You dropped ten stacks just for us to be here?"

Kalil took a deep breath and closed his eyes, as if to jog his memory. "I read a lot in here, considering my extended amount of free time." He grinned slightly. "I came across your novels and loved them. They are authentic. I don't have a lot of time and I wanted to tell someone my story. It really needs to be heard." Kalil alternated stares between the two authors.

"We don't do autobiographies, sorry," JaQuavis replied.

"Look, I know you two are busy and I'm glad that you took out the time to come see me. But what I have to say is something that needs to be heard. I don't have a lot of time," Kalil whispered in an almost desperate tone.

JaQuavis and Ashley exchanged glances and nodded to each other. They then focused their attention back on Kalil.

"I know that you guys write together and that's why I chose to try to contact you two rather than another author. My story is told on two sides. I needed a male and a female to hear what I have to say, nah mean?"

"Who said something about a story, fam? We're not trying—"

"Hold up, I think we should hear him out." Ashley crossed her legs and stared at Kalil. She could tell that he definitely needed to get something off his chest and she figured that since they'd made the trip they might as well see what was up. "Go ahead. We're listening."

"My story is about pain, about love, about"—Kalil stopped to gather himself as the harsh memories formed in his mind—"about love and hate. My story needs to be heard, our story needs to be heard." Kalil lowered his head and covered his face with his hands. He sniffed as he tried to block out his emotions. "London was one of the most beautiful women I had ever laid my eyes on." Then he closed his eyes, and a single tear slid down his cheek. "I remember how it all started. I was just getting out of jail from a four-year stretch."

Chapter One

"Yo, I'm telling you, son, I used to get it out in D.C." June shook his head from side to side as he reminisced. "Nigga, you weren't getting it like that," Kalil taunted the nigga as he bragged.

An exasperated expression crossed June's face as he stood to his feet and replied, "What! Yo, son, I'm trying to put you up on game. I was the man in D.C."

"You were hurting 'em like that? In D.C.? I hear them cats out there ain't working with nothing."

"Man, don't believe that shit. Those D.C. niggas is caked up. They got the money to spend. I was getting crazy-paid out that way. I was fucking with my man from the Midwest. He was giving me the bricks for cheap, so I was making a killing when I resold them in D.C."

"You were traveling all the way west just to cop?" Kalil asked.

"Ain't nobody around the way got that type of weight. I'm telling you, the dude I was dealing with was knee-deep in the game. Right before I got nabbed he was trying to cop like a hundred bricks. Word on the street is he still looking for somebody to fill that order."

Before June had made that statement, Kalil was just having a friendly conversation, but with that one sentence June sparked his interest. June knew that Kalil was connected. There was hearsay around the prison that Kalil had gotten caught with a quarter million when he was arrested, and that he was connected to Hova, Manhattan's most notorious drug lord. Hova wasn't your average kingpin; in fact, it was almost impossible to touch him, which was why Kalil had so much respect. He'd done what other niggas couldn't do. He'd touched the untouchable and become affiliated with Hova. Kalil knew that June was throwing out the bait.

"That could be a payday for *somebody*." June watched Kalil put his belongings into the small box that sat on the top bunk.

"Maybe. I know what you getting at, man, but I ain't fucking with it. That shit ain't worth my freedom. Four years in this mu'fucka is long enough for me to know that I ain't trying to come back. I got a daughter that's waiting on me to come home. I can't leave my family again. Getting money is what I do best, but I can't mess with it right now. I got to find another way to eat, nah mean?"

June nodded his head. He'd left his own son to be raised by his mother, so he could definitely feel where his cellmate was coming from. He didn't like it, because he knew that Kalil was the missing link that he would need when he got out, but for now he had to respect it.

"Kelly, it's time to go," the guard yelled, calling Kalil by his last name. He opened the door and stepped inside the small space and impatiently waited for Kalil to say good-bye and grab his stuff.

June stood up from his bunk and slapped hands with Kalil as they embraced slightly.

"You be easy, duke," Kalil told him.

"I'ma get at you when I get out in a couple months. Maybe by then you'll be ready to step back into the big leagues. Word to my mother, my man on deck for a hundred of 'em. One more time and we can both be set for a minute," June mumbled in Kalil's ear before releasing him.

Kalil nodded. "Get with me when you're free." He grabbed the box that contained his belongings and walked out of the cell as he was guided toward the exit.

The air outside the prison was fresh, and Kalil inhaled deeply as he made his way down the long driveway that led to his freedom. After four years in lockup he was finally going home. His facial hair had grown in abundance and he was in desperate need of a haircut.

The gray rusted-out Cutlass Supreme that was parked at the exit put a smile on his face, and he jogged slightly until he reached the car.

His cousin Quinn jumped out the car as he saw him approach. "What up, baby?" Quinn said as they slapped hands and embraced. "You finally out, mu'fucka. You looking good, still breathing and shit."

"Barely, fam. These past four years have been hard."

Quinn went to the trunk of his car and pulled out a Macy's bag that contained the latest Sean John apparel. He threw it at Kalil. "Get out of that funky-ass jail suit." Quinn walked around to the driver's side and got in. He revved up the engine, and as Kalil hopped in the passenger side, they sped off, leaving skid marks in front of the prison.

Quinn was happy to see Kalil. They'd been close since childhood, and it hurt his heart to see him get sent away. "So how it feel to be out, fam?"

"Damn good, nigga. I just can't wait to see Jada." Kalil thought about his baby girl. She was his world. Out of her eight years on this earth he'd been absent from her life for four of them. He promised himself that he would never miss another minute with her.

"Yeah, she's getting big too. I didn't even tell her that you were getting out today. I figured you should surprise her."

"Thanks for looking out for Destiny while I was down. She raising my daughter and she ain't strong enough to do that by herself. If I couldn't be there, I'm glad that you were."

Kalil and Destiny had been together off and on since high school. When she got pregnant he was a stand-up dude and was there for her. Kalil was a man and he took care of his responsibilities. Destiny and Jada were his world, and he spoiled them both until he got nabbed.

"Man, you family. Ain't no need for all that thank-you bullshit. I did what I had to do to make sure your shorty was straight."

After an awkward silence filled the car, Quinn added, "Yo, open that glove box and hand me that Reasonable Doubt."

Kalil reached for the glove box, and the entire panel fell to the floor. He burst out in laughter as he scooped the CD and the other contents from the floor. "Damn, fam, I've been down for four years and you still ain't copped anything new?"

"You don't know nothing 'bout the Cutlass," Quinn replied with a boyish smirk. He adjusted his side mirrors so that he could see his tires.

Quinn's gray Cutlass Supreme had a few rust spots around the body, and the interior was old, dusty, and worn. It was barely running, but the highlight of the car was the twenty-two-inch rims he had it sitting on.

"Look at them rims, duke. You don't know nothing about that set right there. That's three stacks right there, just on the tires."

Kalil was cracking up as he listened to his little cousin defend his whip. He knew Quinn though, and he was a born hustler with a ridiculous car fetish. He knew that Quinn's pockets had to be hurting for him to be rolling in a broke man's car. It was in their veins to get money, so he didn't understand why Quinn was barely making it.

"But, for real, what's good out here? Money slow or something?"

"The game has changed, man. Ain't nobody really been getting it like that since you went away. Fatboy the only mu'fucka in the city that's doing something."

"Fatboy? That bum-ass nigga?" Kalil knew Fatboy well and couldn't believe that he was now the man on top. Fatboy was a grimy hustler who had no loyalty whatsoever. He was also a known snitch, cooperating with the police on more than one occasion to avoid getting shipped upstate, which was why Kalil and many other hustlers around the city kept him at a distance.

"I'm telling you, can't nobody get they hands on nothing quality. Fatboy the only mu'fucka who got some decent work. I mean his shit ain't the greatest, but it's better than nothing. He stays consistent. He always got work, and you know a nigga got to eat."

"You fucking with him?" Kalil tried to keep the disapproving tone out of his voice, not wanting to knock Quinn's hustle, if in fact he was doing business with Fatboy. On the inside he hoped that Quinn wasn't desperate enough to mess with Fat-boy.

"Hell, nah. I'm trying to stay free. I know if something ever went down, Fatboy would be the first one singing to the cops, so I don't fuck with him. That's why I ain't really messing with the coke right now."

"You should've contacted my man. Hova would've taken care of you." Kalil shook his head. He couldn't believe that Fatboy had taken over the city. Before he went in Fatboy was a clown. He'd tried his hardest to get down with Kalil, but Kalil refused to mess with him. Kalil only dealt with thoroughbreds, and Fatboy was definitely not that.

"Man, Hova ain't messing with nobody but you. He ain't trying to be associated with anybody black. That's why you need to holla at your boy, so we can get back in it." Quinn pulled onto Destiny's street.

Kalil was about to respond, but his words stuck in his throat when he saw the little girl riding her bike in the middle of the street. His eyes were glued to her, and his heartbeat sped up. She was identical to him in every way. Their bronze skin tone was identical, and their almond-shaped eyes were the same shade of dark brown.

Quinn pulled the car toward the curb and parked as Jada ran up to him.

"Uncle Quinn!" she yelled as she bum-rushed him with a hug.

He hugged her back. "I got a surprise for you."

"What is it?" she asked eagerly as she patted his pockets.

Usually he would give her money or jewelry when he came over, so she was excited to see her new gift. Quinn patted his body and snapped his fingers in defeat. "Dang, I think I left it in the car. Go get it from my partner in the passenger seat."

Jada looked toward the car and ran over to the door. "My uncle said you have my"—She couldn't complete her sentence when she saw her father sitting in the car. She hadn't seen him since she was four years old, but she loved him dearly. Although she was very young when he went away, the feeling of security and unconditional love that she felt when she was around her father was something that she would never forget. His face was forever implanted in her mind, and she immediately recognized him.

"Daddy!" she screamed as she jumped into his lap.

Kalil grabbed his daughter and held her tightly as he rocked her back and forth. He stood up out of the car with her still in his arms. "Hey, baby girl," he cooed as she clung on to his neck, her legs wrapped around his body. He could feel tears running from her face.

"I love you, Daddy," she cried. "Don't leave me again. You were gone for a long time."

"Don't worry about nothing, baby girl. I love you so much, I'll never leave you again. Daddy's home to stay."

"You promise?"

"I promise, Jada."

When he placed her gently back on the ground, she ran and hit her Uncle Quinn lightly in the stomach. She yelled, "You kept a secret from me, Uncle Quinn!"

Quinn couldn't help but laugh at her attempts to beat him up. He picked her up and spun her around above his head. "I had to keep it a surprise, big head." He laughed as he put her down.

Kalil looked down at his daughter. She had gotten so big, and he had missed so much time in her life. He smiled as he noticed for the first time what she was wearing. She wore baggy jeans that were twice her size and one of his old Rocawear hoodies that swallowed her tiny frame. Her hair was pulled back in a messy ponytail, and she wore a fitted baseball cap on her head. The last time he'd seen her, she was pretty in pink. Now she was a tomboy.

That's my baby girl, Kalil thought to himself. He knelt in front of his daughter. "Where's your mama?"

"She in the house," Jada replied.

Quinn came up behind Jada and picked her up and put her on his shoulders. He looked at Kalil. "Go handle your business with Destiny. I'll keep an eye on Jada."

Kalil walked into the house and heard Lyfe Jennings's voice coming out of the surround-sound system he'd purchased before he went to prison. He could smell the scent of incense burning, a look of disgrace crossing his face as he looked around the filthy house. Destiny was slipping. She was getting trifling, and he knew he had to straighten her out now that he was home.

As he made his way through the house, he called out, "Des!" His voice was drowned out by the loud music. "This girl got my daughter living in this dirty-ass house," he mumbled as he stepped over pizza boxes and empty Heineken bottles. He tripped over a large pair of boots in the middle of the floor but caught his bearings before he fell. "Damn!" he yelled as he picked up the pair of boots. He frowned when he realized that they were a size twelve. *I know Destiny ain't had a nigga in my house.*

He walked toward her bedroom door, and as soon as he opened it, his suspicions were confirmed. Destiny was on her knees hitting off Fatboy. Stunned to the point of silence, Kalil felt a thousand daggers shoot through his chest.

Fatboy looked up and saw Kalil standing in the doorway, and he nodded as a smirk grew on his face. Fatboy could see the devastation and anger in Kalil's face, and it felt good to be degrading his baby moms right in front of him.

Yeah, nigga, watch me bag your bitch. You ain't on top no more. This my bitch. Fatboy put his hand on the back of Destiny's head and guided it up and down on his shaft. He knew that he was getting the best revenge for all of the times that Kalil had punked him before going to prison. He continued to look at Kalil with a smirk as Destiny gave him the best oral sex of his life. He was grinding into her mouth, one of his hands resting on the back of her head, the other on the pistol that sat near him on the bed.

He felt the orgasm building. "You gon' swallow it for me, ma?"

Before she could answer, he exploded in her mouth and she swallowed it. "Hmm," she moaned.

Kalil shook his head and closed his eyes. He didn't want to believe what he'd just witnessed. His temper quickly began to rise as he opened his eyes. "You dirty bitch," he stated as he laughed lightly. He had to laugh to keep from choking the shit out of her. "You stink-ass bitch!" He hit the wall and turned to leave the room.

"Kalil? Oh my God!" Destiny screamed. "Baby, it's not what it looks like." She rose from her knees and made her way to him.

Kalil couldn't believe that Destiny would pull that tramp shit on him. He had been messing around with her for years, and although he didn't expect her to stay faithful while he was away, he would've never pictured her with Fatboy. Fatboy and Kalil had been adversaries for a long time. Their beef was nothing new, and Destiny was well aware of the history between the two men.

"This nigga? You up in here sucking dick while my daughter outside by herself? You had my daughter around this mu'fucka?" Kalil grabbed her by the neck and shoved her hard against the wall.

Tears fell from Destiny's eyes when she saw the devastated look on Kalil's face.

He pinned her against the wall and punched beside her head, causing her to jump. The pain that he felt from her betrayal surprised even him.

"Wait, Kalil. Baby, I love you. I'm sorry," she shouted as she cried hysterically.

Fatboy smiled as he stood and pulled up his pants. He mugged Kalil as he picked up his Tims and slowly put them on his feet. "Yo' bitch give some good head." Then he peeled off a couple hundred dollars and threw them on the floor. "Thanks for the entertainment, Destiny. Yo' nigga too broke to feed you, so take that money and buy you and your brat something to eat."

Just the mention of his daughter from Fatboy's lips sent him into a different mind state. "What?" Kalil pushed Destiny one last time and then violently lunged for Fatboy.

Fatboy reached for his pistol, but before he could withdraw it from his waistline, Kalil picked up one of the empty Heineken bottles and smashed it across the side of his face.

"Kalil, I'm sorry," Destiny screamed as she watched the two men go blow for blow on her living room floor. "Stop it!" she yelled.

Kalil didn't hear her cries. All he could see was red. He continually raised his fist and brought it down hard over Fatboy's face as he pummeled him, blood spraying across the floor with every punch. He was sure that his hand was broken because he could feel the pain shoot through his arm, but he was relentless in his attack.

Afraid that Kalil would eventually kill Fatboy, Destiny ran outside. "Quinn, help me! They're in here fighting!"

Quinn rushed into the house, with Jada not far behind him. When he walked in, he saw the two men tussling on the floor. He rushed over to Kalil, but instead of stopping the fight, he jumped in. He didn't give a damn about how it started, but he was definitely going to help his boy finish it. They both kicked and stomped at Fatboy. Nobody could save Fatboy from the ass-whupping he was receiving.

The sight of her father and uncle beating on Fatboy and the amount of blood that was covering the white carpet of the living room floor frightened Jada. "Daddy, stop it!"

The sound of Jada's voice snapped Kalil out of his fit of rage. He looked down at Fatboy. He mashed his face in the broken glass as he talked to him, "You bitch nigga, the next time you pull a gun on me, you better squeeze the trigger."

Kalil got up and shook his hand in excruciation. "Fuck!" He held his hand out in front of him and opened and closed his fist repeatedly, to see if he had any serious damage.

"Baby, wait!" Destiny chased after Kalil as he stormed out the house.

Kalil knew that if he turned around, he would haul off and slap the shit out of her, so he ignored her cries. He scooped Jada in his arms and headed for Quinn's car.

"Nigga, where are you going with my daughter? Huh? Kalil!" She followed him all the way to Quinn's car. Kalil turned around and faced her. She could see the look of disgust in his eyes.

"Destiny, I'm done with your ass. I'm taking my daughter with me for a couple days. I'll bring her back when you get your shit together. What the fuck were you thinking? Huh, bitch? You got that mu'fucka all up in my crib, around my daughter?"

Destiny couldn't find a reply. At a time she had desperately loved Kalil. When he was on top of the world and kept her living lavish, she was more than faithful. She never thought about what she would do when he fell from grace, and eventually she began to stray from him. She knew that she was dead wrong. All she could do was stand on the curb sobbing as she watched the car pull away.

Kalil carried Jada up the steps that led to Quinn's small apartment. He laid her down on the couch, turned on the television, and then walked into the kitchen. He opened the freezer door and pulled out the ice tray. "I can't believe Destiny would pull this shit." Kalil submerged his hand in a bowl of ice. "Did you know about them fucking around?"

Quinn shook his head. "Nah. I mean, I've heard things from around the way about them, but I never had proof. I asked her about it once and she denied it, so I took her word as bond. I didn't want to tell you no bullshit that would have your head fucked up in prison, so I just kept it at that."

Kalil looked toward the living room where his daughter rested. "She so busy sucking that fat nigga dick that she can't teach my daughter how to be a lady. She dressing like a boy and shit, running around here with her hair all wild." He took a deep breath, trying to calm himself down. "I can't go back there, yo, because the way I feel right now, I'll kill her, Quinn."

Quinn knew how much Kalil had cared for Destiny. When Kalil had first met her she was spoiled. She assumed the position of street royalty because Kalil was the king of the streets. Destiny's stock went up just by associating with Kalil, but without him she had gone back to being just another hood rat.

"Bro, don't trip off that shit. You and Destiny been going through bullshit like this since you met her. It's time to let that go. You can crash here at the cut as long as you need. It'll be like the old days."

"Thanks, man. I swear I'll come up with some dough. I won't be down for long."

Quinn's cell phone rang loudly, interrupting their conversation. He looked down at his caller ID and announced, "It's Destiny, man."

Kalil shook his head and then reached for the phone. "Yeah," he answered.

"Kalil? Kalil, look, it's not what it looked like. I love you, baby. I swear I was just lonely."

Kalil rubbed his temple as he exhaled deeply. He had been through this same song and dance with his baby mama before. She would fuck around, get caught, and he would listen to her excuses and then forgive her. In the past he accepted that because he knew that it came with the territory of having a child out of wedlock.

Destiny was the mother of his child so he figured he would have to tolerate her bullshit, but their current situation was different. She'd crossed the line, and there was no going back. She knew that he had beef with Fatboy and she still chose to fuck around with him. She wasn't loyal, and that wasn't something he was willing to forgive.

Her ass didn't know that I was coming home this soon. She probably thought that I would never find out, he thought as he held the phone in his hands.

Destiny was crying and lying into the phone, but he wasn't trying to hear it. There was nothing that she could say to make him change his mind about her now. She was nothing more than a ho to him now. She'd dug her own grave. Now she had to lie in it.

"Des, I'm not doing this with you anymore."

"What you mean? Why are you doing this to me?"

Kalil couldn't help but laugh at her. *This bitch must be out of her damn mind*. He wasn't about to let her flip the situation and make him think that he was in the wrong. He was very familiar with her art of seduction and manipulation, having fallen for her tears time and time again.

"Des, you did this to yourself. I'm through with you. I'm not fucking with you anymore.

That shit you pulled today was more than I can handle. I need a woman that will hold me down, not some trick that will chase behind any nigga that throw a little bit of money her way. You're lucky that I'm taking this shit as well as I am. I should've killed your ass, but I know that you don't know any better. This is just how you are. You do fucked-up shit and you don't care who you hurt in the process. The worse part about it is that you don't learn from the shit, Des. You keep making the same mistakes over and over again. I can't change you, no matter how much I want to. A ho gon' always be a ho. I should've never tried to turn you into wifey. It's not in your nature to be a classy chick."

"You can't just drop me, Kalil. What am I supposed to do? What about your daughter?"

"You dropped yourself when you started fucking with that chump nigga. You are no longer a concern of mine. Don't call me for money and don't come searching for me when that mu'fucka start lumping your shit up. I am done with you." He could hear her crying, and it almost wore him down. He didn't know if she was really hurt or if she was acting. She knew that he hated to see her cry and he almost gave in, but every time he even thought about forgiving her, he thought about Fatboy guiding her mouth onto his dick.

"I love you, Kalil. What about Jada?"

"You should have thought about how much you loved me before you got on your knees for that nigga. My daughter doesn't have shit to do with this. I'm gon' always be there for her. She is my life, and I will never turn my back on her. You know that I will give her whatever she needs. You, on the other hand, you are no longer my responsibility. You better have Fatboy take care of you." He hung up the phone and turned it off, knowing that if he didn't she would blow him up the entire night.

"See you in the morning, fam," Kalil said to Quinn as he joined Jada in the living room. He sat on the floor next to Jada and watched her sleep peacefully. He smiled at how beautiful she looked. Just the sight of her made him forget about everything that had happened earlier. He rubbed the top of her head softly and nestled his nose against her cheek. She shifted in her sleep and opened her eyes.

"What's wrong, Daddy?" She placed her small hand on top of his head then patted it lightly.

Kalil laughed. "Nothing, baby girl. Nothing's wrong. I was just watching you sleep. You know you snore like a pig, right?"

Jada's eyes got big from embarrassment and she shook her head and laughed. "Uh-uh! No, I don't."

Kalil kissed his daughter's cheek and admired her features. She was a perfect blend of Kalil and Destiny. *One thing Destiny did do right is give me a beautiful baby girl.*

"I'm glad you're home, Daddy," Jada said, interrupting his thoughts. "Can I come live with you and Uncle Quinn?"

Kalil wanted nothing more than to have his daughter come live with him, but he had to get his money up and get his own place first. "Not yet, Jada. I need to get my own spot first, but I promise that we'll be together soon. Until then I will come see you every day."

"You promise?" she asked, tears in her eyes.

"I promise."

Jada gave him the most serious face that her eight-year-old mind could muster and then held up her pinky.

He already knew what that meant, so he held up his pinky and said, "I pinky-swear, baby girl. Now get some sleep." He kissed her on top of her head, and they both rested their minds for the night.

Chapter Two

Jada tried to get Kalil out of his deep sleep. "Wake up, Daddy, wake up!" Her attempts were useless, so she stuck her finger up his nose.

Kalil opened his eyes and saw his daughter laughing at him.

"Wake up, sleepyhead. I have to go to school." Jada jumped on top of her father's back and began to bounce on him, trying to get him to get up.

He briefly pulled his head from underneath the pillow. "Baby girl, you can miss school today. Just let Daddy get ten more minutes." The only thing on Kalil's mind was sleep. It had been so long since he'd been able to sleep in. Being locked up, he was always on somebody else's schedule.

"I have to go to school. Get up!" Jada said as she hopped off of Kalil. "If I miss school, I can't go to dance class after."

Kalil realized that he had no choice but to get up. "I'm up, baby girl, I'm up," he mumbled groggily as he sat up slowly. "Go and get ready."

Jada didn't move. She put her hands on her hips and said, "Mommy always does my hair before I go to school."

Kalil glanced at Jada's hair and noticed it was a complete mess. Even then, she was the most beautiful girl in the world to him. He didn't know the first thing about doing hair.

"Come on, sleepyhead." Jada grabbed Kalil's hand and tried to pull him up, but Kalil playfully pulled her onto the couch and began to tickle her.

After a couple of minutes of playing, Kalil finally got up and focused on the big task ahead—getting his eight-year-old ready for school.

Kalil patted Jada's big sandy-brown Afro. "What are we going to do with this hair?"

He suddenly got an idea. Without even putting on shoes, he headed out of the door and went across the hall to Roxi's place and knocked on the door. After seconds of waiting, he finally heard her voice.

"Who is it?"

"It's Kalil."

"Kalil?" Roxi said in surprise as she stood on the opposite side of the door. She slowly opened it up and saw her childhood crush on her doorstep. She knew that he would eventually come to his senses and try to push up on her. She smiled like a child. Just the thought of him made her love box thump. *This sexy-ass nigga knocking on my door this early in the morning. I knew he would come around.* She loosened her grip on her robe, suggestively showing Kalil her bra-and-panty set. The cold air made her nipples instantly hard, and to her surprise, Kalil's eyes stayed above her neck.

"Hey, Kalil, how may I help you?" she said in her sexiest bedroom voice.

"What up, Roxi? Sorry to bother you, but I got a little problem that I need you to help me with."

Roxi's face lit up. This was the day she'd waited for since she was a little girl. "Whatever you want, Kalil."

Kalil grew a blank look on his face as he realized Roxi's intentions. He didn't want to embarrass her, so he just got to the point. "I got my daughter across the hall, and she's got to be at school in an hour. I would really appreciate if—"

"Say no more. I got you, Kalil. How old is she?" She was disappointed, but would still help Kalil out. *This man ain't never noticed you before, so he ain't about to start now,* she told herself as she waited for Kalil to reply.

"She's eight."

"My little sister is about her age. I'll be over there after I put on some clothes," she said, slightly embarrassed. *I can't believe I came at him all desperate. What was I thinking?*

"Thanks, ma. I owe you," Kalil said as he returned to Quinn's apartment.

Five minutes later Roxi came over and did Jada's hair and gave her some of her sister's clothes to wear to school. Kalil looked at his beautiful daughter and was glad that she had taken off those boyish clothes. He finally had his daughter back.

Eight Hours Later

"Yo, this is some bullshit," Kalil said as he walked through the door and loosened his tie.

"No luck, fam?" Quinn licked the blunt, preparing to split it.

"Nobody is trying to hire a black ex-con. I can't catch a break for shit. I've had five interviews today, and because of my record, they all turned me down." Kalil flopped down on the couch in frustration.

Quinn took a long pull of the blunt he had in his mouth and answered while the smoke was still in his lungs. "I don't know why you are stressing over a bullshit job. The answer to all your problems is in Manhattan, fam."

Kalil knew exactly what Quinn was referring to, but he vowed he would never go that route again.

Quinn continued, "You should go and holla at Hova and get put back in the game. That's where the money at."

"I am not going back to the streets. I already have two strikes, and if I get knocked again, it's over for me. I couldn't put Jada through that, not again."

"I respect your decision, but all I ever known you to be was a hustler." Quinn took another drag of his blunt and shook his head from side to side. "Remember when Hova hit you with that weight? Man, we made over a hundred thousand in a month span. That was living right there. We could take over the game. That shit Fatboy putting in the streets is garbage. If the hood gets a taste of Hova's product, we could really make some noise. Just think about it, Kalil."

"I'm not fucking with it, Quinn. I'm out for good," Kalil said, agitation in his voice this time.

Quinn decided to give it up. He knew that it was no use trying to persuade his cousin, so he changed the subject. "You need to get out and have some fun, my nigga. Let's hit this new club in Manhattan tonight called Club Heaven. All the finest shorties in the city be in there."

"No doubt. I need to get out anyway."

Just then the house phone rang. Quinn picked up the phone and glanced at the caller ID. "Yo, fam, it's Destiny. She's been calling my phone all day." He handed Kalil the cordless phone.

"Hello," Kalil answered with a sigh.

Destiny's voice blared through the phone. "Where the fuck you been, Kalil? I've been calling you all day."

"Here you go with that shit." Kalil shook his head, preparing for the drama.

"Nigga, fuck you! Bring Jada back home, Kalil. Who the fuck do you think you are?"

"Who you talking to like that? You better remember who the fuck you talking to. You had Fatboy dick in yo' mouth when you were supposed to be watching my baby. Anything could've happened to her while you were—"

"Nigga, you ain't shit no more!" Destiny yelled into the phone. "You ain't getting any money! Yo' broke ass is over there at Quinn's house doing nothing. Maybe Fatboy can show you a thang or two 'bout getting paper. You's a mu'fuckin' has-been. Ol' sorry, no-good-fa-nothin' nigga!"

Kalil didn't know what to say to Destiny. She had never talked to him like that. Since he had been locked up, she had gotten real disrespectful. He knew she could never be his chick again. No woman should talk to her man that way. He remembered the days when she worshipped the ground he walked on. As he sat and listened to her bitch, he realized that it was the money that she loved. His pride was crushed.

"Look, Des, I will bring Jada home on Sunday. Just let me keep her for the weekend. I ain't seen my shorty in years. We got some catching up to do," Kalil stated in a calm tone, trying to keep the peace with her.

"Whatever. You make sure you take my baby to dance practice today. She has to go every day and don't have any bitches around my—"

Before she could even finish her bickering, Kalil introduced her to the dial tone. He glanced at the clock on the wall. "Oh shit, I have to go pick up Jada." With that, he rushed out to retrieve his daughter from school.

Kalil had spent the entire day with Jada and gave her his undivided attention. They watched all of Jada's favorite Disney movies.

Although Kalil didn't show it, Destiny's words had gotten to him. He wasn't used to not having money. Every time he thought about getting back into the drug game, the sight of Jada enjoying his company altered his decision. *I have to be here for her, I have to. Fuck it, I'll work at a fast-food joint before I put my freedom at stake again.*

Kalil watched Jada nod off on the couch next to him. He gently kissed her on the top of her head and put a blanket over her. He turned off the movie and prepared to get ready for his night out. Roxi had agreed to come over and keep an eye on Jada while he and Quinn went to the club. Kalil tip toed out the door to go and get Roxi, and moments later returned with her and prepared to get ready for his night out.

***

Kalil and Quinn bobbed their heads to the music as they pulled up to the downtown Manhattan club. The club was packed, and the line wrapped around the corner. "Damn, it's jumping in there." Kalil leaned forward in his seat to get a better view.

"I told you, son, this is the spot right here."

They parked the car and hopped out. Quinn had on a cocaine-white Sean Jean leather jacket and wore butter Tims on his feet, overshadowing his cousin, who wore a black hoodie with jeans and definitely didn't look like his old self.

Years back Kalil always wore the flyest shit. Now he felt naked without a Jesus piece around his neck.

Quinn didn't say it, but it kind of felt good to finally outshine his cousin. Their roles had totally switched.

Even though Kalil wasn't dressed like a boss, in his mind he still was one. He wasn't dressed to impress, but no one could take his swagger away from him. Quinn had offered him some of his clothes, but he had too much pride to be rocking another man's gear.

As they approached the line, Kalil heard someone call his name from the front. It was Peanut, his old worker.

"Yo, Kalil! What up, my nigga?" Peanut, the doorman to the club, held a clipboard in his hand.

"Yo, what's good, son?" Kalil smiled and threw his hands up.

"Come on, son, you don't have to wait in line." Peanut waved Kalil toward him.

Kalil and Quinn stepped out of line and headed to the front. Kalil and Peanut locked hands and gave each other a brief embrace. Kalil stared at Peanut and noticed he had grown since the last time he'd seen him. He used to be a scrawny, seventeen-year-old corner boy before Kalil went in the joint. Now he had grown facial hair and bulked up. He used to push "blow" for Kalil and was known to bust his gun. Peanut laid his murder game down even as a young kid, and Kalil had respect for his little man.

"My nigga, when you get out?"

"I just touched down, nah mean?" Kalil said in a strong New York accent.

"No doubt. Yo, Hova's going to be happy to see you. He's upstairs." Peanut opened the club door to let them in.

Kalil had a look of confusion on his face. He knew that Hova was slipping. A powerful man like that shouldn't be in a packed club like Heaven. "Yo, my man Hova in there?"

"Yeah, he owns this joint," Peanut answered.

It all began to make sense to Kalil. He frowned and looked at his cousin. He realized it wasn't a coincidence that Quinn had suggested that particular club.

Quinn wanted Kalil to get back in with Hova for his own personal reasons. He was trying to get back in the dope game, and Kalil's connection with Hova was his key. He gave Kalil a cheesy grin and threw both of his hands up. "What?"

"You knew this was Hova's club, nigga."

Quinn threw his arm around Kalil's neck and guided him into the club. "Yo, cuz, let's just have some fun."

Kalil was upset, but he wasn't going to fuck up the night. "All right, fam, let's have some fun." He gave Quinn a forced grin.

As soon as they entered the building, the luxurious club captivated them. It was simply immaculate. The floors were made of marble, and the whole club had a "heavenly" theme. Beautiful women dressed in seductive angel outfits danced in secluded cages that hung from the club's ceiling. The walls were painted with clouds, and the place was lined with white couches. The club had three different floors, all playing different music. Kalil was definitely impressed.

Kalil and Quinn walked through the crowd, which parted like the Red Sea. Kalil definitely had a presence in the building. He must have slapped about fifty people's hands. He grew uncomfortable because every time someone approached him they looked at his wardrobe in confusion. It was a known fact that Kalil used to shut the club down with the best jewels and latest fashions.

He and Quinn found a booth in the back with a clear view of the dance floor. Kalil watched as the assorted ladies moved their bodies seductively to R. Kelly's hit song. Four years of jail had him on an ass drought, so naturally he caught a wood. As they slid into the booth, Kalil asked, "Is it me, or is every chick in here a dime piece?"

"That's that four years of jail talking. Anything probably looks good to you right now." Quinn called over a waiter and ordered a bottle of champagne and continued to converse with his cousin.

In the middle of their conversation, Peanut approached their table with a bottle of Dom in his hand. Kalil checked out his former worker and realized how much he had stepped his game up. The iced-out pinky ring and the Jesus piece on his necklace had to easily cost him around ten stacks.

Kalil respected it and knew that he was only following in his footsteps. Kalil ran the streets before he got locked up. If he didn't have anything else, he knew he had respect in the streets. He had put in too much work not to.

Peanut sat the bottle on the table and leaned toward Kalil so he could hear him over the music. "Yo, Hova sent you this bottle. He heard you were down here and wants you to come up and holla at him."

Kalil really didn't want to see Hova because he knew the conversation was going to lead to street business, something that Kalil wanted no part of. Every time he thought about entering the drug game and potentially leaving his daughter again, he turned cold toward the streets, but out of respect for Hova, he decided to talk to him.

"No doubt. Where he at?"

Peanut looked at the upper level and pointed to the glass office overlooking the club. Kalil followed his finger and saw Hova overlooking the club with both of his hands behind his back. Kalil took a drink of the Dom and then leaned over to Quinn to tell him that he was about to have a word with Hova and would return shortly.

Quinn nodded his head nonchalantly, but on the inside he was beaming. As Kalil got up and headed toward the wraparound stairs, Quinn began to rub his hands together, thinking about the money they were about to get. *Kalil is a mu'fuckin' hustler. He's going to get back in the game. That hustler's ambition is going to kick in sooner or later.*

Chapter Three

Kalil sat in front of Hova and his crew, better known as his twelve disciples. Kalil could feel the tension in the room as Hova's disciples tried to read him. He sat and waited for Hova to speak. Hova's stare was intense, but Kalil wasn't intimidated. He knew that they had unfinished business, but what he didn't know was whether he was in good or bad standing with the stone-faced white man sitting in front of him. Hova's aqua blue eyes scanned the room as he sat back in his leather chair, his legs crossed. His blond hair and tan skin would make most men underestimate him. However, Kalil wasn't one of those men. He'd witnessed firsthand the repercussions of go-ing against the grain and was well aware that Hova was a killer. In fact, he was a cold-blooded murderer. He could touch whoever he wanted to, and Kalil had heard of him murdering innocent women and children just to prove himself to his majority black clientele.

Bottom line, most people didn't want to be made an example by Hova. He didn't have love in New York, he didn't receive love from the streets—he was feared by them. That was what separated him from his competition. He didn't seek the street fame. He wanted people to fear him, and most did, but Kalil was one of the few men who didn't.

"Give us a little bit of privacy," Hova said to his loyal disciples.

The men walked out slowly while Hova and Kalil eyed each other intensely. Kalil shifted in his seat. It had been four years since he'd last seen Hova, and the silence in the room was beginning to make him uncomfortable. Kalil was naked in the club. He wasn't strapped that night because he knew that he couldn't bring his gun inside. He was well aware of Hova's tactics and knew that there were weapons stashed in various spots around the room, and that if they'd had beef for whatever reason, he would've been in trouble.

Hova got up and walked over to the sixty-inch plasma television that hung on his office wall and pressed a red button. The TV lifted, revealing a loaded minibar behind it. "You want a drink?" Hova poured himself a glass of cognac.

"Nah, I'm good," Kalil replied.

"I heard about the deal that you were offered."
Hova took a sip of the yak (cognac). "I appreciate
your loyalty."

"I got myself into that situation. Wasn't no
point in pulling another man down with me, nah
mean?"

Hova nodded his head and paced around the
room as if he were contemplating a big decision.
He pointed a finger at Kalil. "You see, that's why
we get along—we understand this business." He
went over to the bar and pressed the red button
again, but this time, instead of the TV sliding
back into place, a safe came into view. Hova
discreetly entered the combination and opened
the safe, revealing the gold mine inside.

Hova removed a 9 mm pistol and four kilos
of cocaine from the safe. He sat the items in
front of Kalil and watched as Kalil's eyes danced
curiously on the objects in front of him. "It's
good to have you home, Kalil. That right there
is everything that you need to take back what is
yours. We can easily put our business together
back in motion. Just say the word."

Damn! I could flip this. Kalil picked up the
gun and admired the chrome. He quickly put
it down and slid it back across the table toward
Hova. "Thanks, man. It feels good to be home. I

don't have too much use for that, though," Kalil stated. "I'm trying to keep my hands clean, you know?"

"You're a smart man. Never make the same mistake twice."

Kalil nodded to acknowledge what Hova had said.

"Well, when you're ready to step back into the game, I'll be here. There is a lot of new money to be made in New York. I'll even give them to you at a discount, to show my appreciation."

Kalil thought about the money and seriously contemplated Hova's proposition. "What type of discount we talking?"

"Twelve a joint."

Hova was practically giving Kalil the weight, considering he charged everybody else he dealt with $19,000 per kilo. Thoughts of luxury living quickly filled Kalil's head, but they were just as quickly replaced with thoughts of his daughter's face.

"Nah, Hov, I'm gon' fall back for a minute. I just got home, so I'm trying to lay low for a while."

"You know I had to give it a shot. You copped more than all of my other clients put together." Hova stood and walked to the two-way mirror, which allowed him to see the dance floor beneath him. He pulled a platinum cigar case from his pocket and removed a Cuban cigar, which he held between his fingers as he talked. "Well, I'll tell you what, you know how to contact me. You call me when you're ready to get your feet wet again. If you need anything, just let me know and it's done."

Kalil stood and shook hands with Hova before he exited the room. He shook his head in astonishment as he walked back down to the main floor of the club was. *Damn, twelve a fucking kilo and I ain't trying to fuck with it?* Kalil felt like a fool for walking away from a deal like that.

He located Quinn by the bar, where he was kicking game to some chick. He approached him and waited until he was done speaking with the female before he said, "Let's get up out of here.".

"Everything all right, fam?" Quinn asked, ready to handle any beef that may have surfaced.

"Yeah, everything's one hundred, man. I just want to scoop Jada before she drives Roxi crazy."

Quinn ditched the chick he was kicking it with, and they walked out of the club. He was eager to hear what happened in Hova's office. "What did Hov have to say?"

"Not much. He just welcomed me home."

Kalil knew that Quinn would call him crazy for turning down Hova's proposition. He turned up

the stereo as 50 Cent's debut CD pumped through
the speakers. Kalil and Quinn still bobbed their
heads to the classic song, "Many Men," and rode
in silence the rest of the way home.

"Bye, Daddy!" Jada yelled as she ran into
school the next day. She had been attending the
performing arts school since kindergarten and
she loved it. Before she got to the entrance she
ran back to her father, who was standing on the
curb. "I love you. Don't forget about my dance
lessons after school."

Kalil kneeled so they could be eye to eye. He
took his thumb and cleaned some leftover sleep
out of her eye. "What time you get out?"

"Five o'clock. You're going to pick me up,
right, Daddy?"

"Yeah, I'll be here. Be good today, baby girl."
He kissed the top of her head, and she ran off
with a huge smile on her face.

Kalil began to walk back toward Quinn's house.
Quinn had some business to take care of, so Kalil
had to walk Jada to school that morning. It wasn't
a big deal, since Quinn only lived six blocks from
Jada's school, but it was embarrassing, to say the
least.

Kalil was used to being on top. In his twenty-seven years, he'd earned hundreds of thousands of dollars, and there was a time when he could get anything he wanted. Those times were long gone, though, and he was having a hard time adapting to his newfound struggle. He wanted to do the right thing. He was trying his hardest to walk a straight line and stay out of the game, but nobody was willing to give him a break. *I just need a job, yo, for real. I can't stay down like this for too much longer.* He knew that he had to take care of his daughter. He refused to let her go without and realized that the older she got, the more she'd need. He wanted to be able to give her the world and more.

As he walked back to Quinn's house, he noticed the construction zone that took up an entire block, and the sign: EXPERIENCED WORKERS NEEDED—$24/HOUR. He looked up at the large half-constructed buildings and decided that he didn't have anything to lose. He needed a job, and if this was a paying gig, he was willing to do it. He walked into the construction zone and made his way to the trailer that sat in the middle of all the ruckus and knocked loudly.

Someone shouted, "Come on in!"

Kalil stepped inside the office and saw a short man sitting behind a desk and puffing on a cigar.

The man looked up from the paperwork that sat in front of him, his deep brow wrinkled in a frown. "Who the fuck are you?" he asked in his Italian accent.

"I'm here to apply for the job."

The man looked Kalil up and down. "Apply for the job, huh. Do you have any experience?"

"Yeah, I'm familiar with this type of work. I did some construction in Jersey some years back," he lied.

The man continued to eye Kalil with contempt. It was almost as if he looked down at Kalil, like he thought he was better than him. But Kalil ignored the man's degrading demeanor. He was just looking for a job.

"We really need some help around here. Think you can handle it?" The man pointed his cigar at Kalil, waiting for an answer.

"Yeah, I know how to do the job," Kalil replied through gritted teeth. He could tell that the man didn't like him much, but he didn't care. He needed to make some money, and this job was his last option. Quinn was being very understanding by letting him crash at his spot, but Kalil didn't like to depend on anybody for anything, even if it was family.

"What's your name, boy?"

"Kalil," he replied, shifting his stance uncomfortably. He didn't appreciate the man's blatant disregard, but he bit his tongue. "Yo, do you got room for me or not?"

The man looked at him harshly. He didn't like Kalil. In fact, he didn't like anybody whose skin was darker than a temporary suntan, but he needed workers.

Just from the looks of Kalil he could tell that he wasn't a part of a union, which meant he didn't have to pay him union wages. His eyes scanned the young man before him. He quickly noticed the jailhouse tattoos on Kalil's arms and smirked to himself. He could sense Kalil's desperation. Since nobody in New York was trying to hire an ex-con, he knew Kalil would accept the bogus offer that he was about to make.

I'll pay him peanuts just to get this project done. He rose from his desk. "Look, kid, I don't usually hire your people, especially since you got a record, but I'm going to give you a shot. You start today. Be on time, and don't come in here with your baggy pants and your fucking black slang. My name is Mr. Moretti, and don't ask me any fucking questions. You keep up with the other men, then maybe—just maybe—I'll keep you on board. You'll make thirteen dollars an hour. Here, fill out this application."

At the sound of Moretti's name, Kalil instantly knew who he was. The Moretti family was infamous in Manhattan for their extortion and cocaine business. He knew that the construction company had to be a front business. He remembered back when he was Moretti's competition. Now he was trying to be his employee. *Ain't this about a bitch, Kalil thought.* "Thirteen dollars? The sign out front says twenty-four."

"The sign out front is for good Italian men. I know your type. You've got to find a job to keep the parole officer off your ass. I'll help you out, but we do this on my terms. You I pay thirteen dollars. Take it or leave it," the fat man huffed.

If this had happened a couple years earlier Kalil would have left the man slumping in the gutter, but those days were long gone. Now he was broke and just trying to raise a little girl. He had to accept the job, wack wages and all.

"I'll take it."

Kalil filled out the application and threw it on Mr. Moretti's desk. Then he walked out of the office and looked around the construction site before hesitantly making his way over to a cement truck. He stood around and watched the men work.

"Why are you just standing around?" one of the foremen yelled to him as he struggled with a long metal beam. "Give me a hand with this."

Kalil grabbed one end of the beam, and the two men spread wet cement evenly across the ground. That was just the beginning of a long and exhausting day.

Kalil worked for nine straight hours in the beaming sun, cement and sweat covering his shirt. For the first time in his life he experienced a hard day's work. Money usually came very easy to him, so hard labor was an eye-opener for him. *Damn! Man, I been working all fucking day and I only made a hundred dollars. This shit ain't worth it.*

Exhausted, he stopped to take a break. He walked into the boss' trailer to grab some water and noticed the time. *Damn! I forgot about Jada.* He took off the borrowed hard hat and tossed it to the ground, rushed out the door, and took off in a sprint to get to his daughter's school.

He arrived there around six o'clock and found it almost deserted. *I was supposed to be here an hour ago.* He entered the school and could hear the sound of classical music coming from the auditorium. He was hoping that the class had run late so that Jada wouldn't think he'd forgotten about her. He walked into the auditorium and stopped as his breath caught in his throat at the sight of the woman onstage, her dark brown skin tone glistening from the sweat that had formed on her body, and her long chestnut-colored hair swinging wildly as she danced across the stage in her black leotard and ballerina shoes.

Kalil had never seen a ballerina before, but he figured that the woman before him had to be the best. The way she moved her body was nothing short of amazing. Almost hypnotic. He quietly took a seat at the back of the auditorium, making sure not to disturb her. He watched her slender, flexible body spin and bend to the violins in the music. He couldn't help but stare at her. There was a passion in the way she danced that intrigued him. Not to mention, she was one of the most beautiful women he'd ever seen. An exotic beauty, she wasn't your average around-the-way–type girl, but seemed to be filled with class and elegance. And there was a sophisticated sparkle in her eye.

The music became more intense, and finally she ended her dance with a dramatic fall to the stage. It was almost like she was crying through her performance. Kalil cleared his throat and rose from his seat.

His presence startled her, and she jumped up in embarrassment and made her way to the sound system that contained the CD she'd just danced to.

"I'm sorry, ma. I didn't mean to scare you," he said as he walked to the edge of the stage. It wasn't until she turned around that he recognized her. It was the same girl that he'd seen in the club a couple nights before.

"My name's not *ma,* it's London. And don't worry about it, you didn't scare me," she said with an attitude.

Kalil could hear the island accent that graced her pretty lips. He stared at her for a minute, causing her to blush and look away.

"Is there something that I can do for you?" She looked him up and down, taking in his dirty appearance. She frowned as she waited for him to reply. "Excuse me," she said, snapping him out of his trance.

"Oh yeah, my daughter Jada. I'm here to pick her up. I know I'm a little late, but I just got off work."

"Well, Jada's already been picked up." London slipped on a sweater that hung loosely over her right shoulder and pulled her hair up into a long ponytail before she continued. "I called her mother about a half-hour ago, and she sent someone to get her. I thought it was her father, but now that I've met you, I guess he must have been a friend of the family."

"What! Who picked her up?" Kalil didn't mean to yell, but just the thought of Fatboy picking up his daughter had him enraged.

London frowned. She wanted to tell him to check his tone, but it was obvious that he was worried about his child, so she let it go. "Let me grab the sign-out log. He had to sign it to get her. I've seen his face before, so I'm sure everything's okay." She dug through her gym bag and pulled out a clipboard.

Kalil scanned the list until he affirmed what he already knew. Fatboy's name was written in sloppy handwriting next to Jada's.

"Is everything okay?"

Kalil didn't even respond to her question. He rushed out of the gym and ran most of the way to Quinn's house.

He quickly borrowed Quinn's car and drove over to Destiny's. He didn't see Fatboy's car outside. He didn't even bother to knock before entering the house. He barged in and slammed the door behind him. "Jada!" he yelled as he pushed past Destiny.

"Fuck you doing?" she asked as she walked behind him.

"If something happens to her, I'm gon' kill you." Kalil pointed his finger in her face and pushed her aside.

"Nigga, what is you talking about?" she yelled. "Don't be coming up in here starting no shit!"

"Where is my daughter?" he yelled.

Jada emerged from her room, still wearing her pink leotard. "I'm right here, Daddy."

He bent down and picked her up as he hugged her tightly.

"Daddy, you're squeezing me too tight."

Jada laughed as Kalil continued to hold her. He leaned back to make sure that every single hair was in place on her head. His dirty hand caressed her youthful cheeks.

Jada could see the tears that had formed in his eyes. "Daddy, you're getting my clothes dirty," she whined.

Kalil kissed her on the cheek and put her down. "I'm sorry. Daddy will get it cleaned for you. Go to your room, baby girl."

Destiny was standing in the middle of the kitchen with her hand on her hips. She didn't have a clue as to why he'd come in her crib tripping.

"Keep that nigga away from my daughter."

"Kalil, why are you tripping? If you were there to pick her up like I told you, I wouldn't have had to call Fatboy to pick her up."

"What the fuck were you thinking? Don't have that nigga around my daughter! You don't know shit about that mu'fucka. He got beef with niggas from all over and you got Jada out here riding with him like she's his shorty. That ain't his seed," Kalil yelled, "she's mine."

"Kalil, please . . . ain't nobody trying to take your place. He doesn't want to be Jada's daddy."

"You don't think, Destiny. Damn! It wasn't too long ago that I almost had that nigga put to sleep. What if some shit popped off while she was with him? What if she got hit by a stray bullet behind some beef that stupid mu'fucka got? Huh? You think you're so smart. You ain't in the streets. You don't know shit about Fatboy, besides what his dick look like. Keep him away from Jada."

"You are really tripping right now. Her dance instructor called and said that my baby was still at the school, so I sent Fatboy to pick her up. Ain't shit happened to her yet. I been taking care of her just fine without you, so don't be trying to flip on me about how I take care of her now." Destiny mumbled to herself, "Nigga wanna come home trying to play daddy," and flipped her hand, signaling that she was done with the conversation.

Before storming out of the house, Kalil said, "You heard what I said, Destiny—Keep his ass away from my daughter before I kill him!"

Destiny followed him to the door. "Well, make sure your ass is on time tomorrow, since your little girl is too precious to get a ride from anybody else!"

Chapter Four

Kalil finished his morning routine and walked into the living room, where Quinn, a blunt hanging out of his mouth, was playing Xbox. Kalil walked past him, and without exchanging words, they smacked palms.

Kalil headed straight for the kitchen to get something to eat. He glanced over at the calendar on the fridge and noticed today was the day he had to see his parole officer. "Damn, I almost forgot about that shit," he said to himself as he fixed himself a bowl of cereal.

Kalil dreaded going to work, but he had to. It was the only thing he could do to make some money. The only true skill he'd acquired over the years was the ability to hustle; that's all he knew. And if that was taken from him, he'd be left naked. Destiny had run through the money that he had stashed away for a rainy day while he was still locked up, so he was back to square one.

Quinn had offered him a partnership in his weed hustle, but Kalil had been in the game long enough to know that this was a dead end. Quinn had been selling weed for five years and was still in the same position, living in the same projects, driving the same car. To Kalil the risk outweighed the reward, so he passed.

Kalil returned to the living room with a big bowl of Frosted Flakes in his hands. "Fam, I got to go and see my P.O. today. Will you shoot me up there?"

"I can't do it. I got some money coming through today, so I got to stay put. Here you go." Quinn dug in his pockets to search for his keys. He pulled them out and tossed them to Kalil. The keys landed right in his cereal.

Kalil was agitated, but he couldn't help but laugh. They both chuckled at the incident, and then Kalil prepared to take off.

He drove down the highway rapping along with Jay-Z's song. The song reminded Kalil of his old hustler's mentality.

Home for only two weeks, he'd repeatedly contemplated visiting his old connect. He knew all he had to do was say the word and Hova would bless him with some bricks of the East Coast's best cocaine. He'd done four years and had never once mentioned Hova's name. The thought of snitching never crossed his mind. He was facing twenty years for the coke he was caught with, but an illegal search hindered the prosecution's case. Instead of the intent to distribute charge, he ended up being sentenced for four to six years for possession. Every time he thought of returning to the streets, he kept thinking about Jada. He vowed not to leave her side again. He wanted to make things right and be a father to her.

Kalil glanced at the clock on the CD player and noticed he had an hour to kill before seeing his parole officer, so he decided to go see Jada. He turned off the highway and headed toward Destiny's house. When he pulled up to the house, he saw a Benz in the driveway. He knew whose car it was by the plates, which read FATBOY.

Just before Kalil parked on the curb, out came Fatboy. He didn't even notice Kalil, but the slamming door caught his attention. The two men's eyes locked, and they both stared at each other intensely. Fatboy threw both of his arms up. He then pulled up his black T-shirt, exposing the rolls in his belly, and his chrome .45.

Kalil already knew what time it was. He didn't have a gun and didn't want anything to pop off. He just said, "I'll see you in the streets, homeboy."

"That's what I thought." Fatboy smirked and got into his Benz, satisfied that he'd just belittled Kalil.

Kalil waited until Fatboy pulled off and then entered the house. *I'm going to get at his fat ass.* As soon as he pushed open the cracked door, the smell of sex crept through his nose. He made his way back to Destiny's room. He opened the door and saw her naked body sprawled across the bed, her bald vagina in clear view as she lightly snored. He still admired her perfect bronze body and loved the way she kept her "lil' mama" shaved. He was tempted to hit it, but he knew the drama that would come along with that. He knew if he had sex with her, she would think that things were back to normal and he didn't want to mislead her, knowing how attached she could get.

Kalil shook his head and closed the door. He heard the television playing in his daughter's room and headed toward the noise. He poked his head in her room and whispered, "Hey, baby girl." He didn't see his daughter, so he stepped inside the room. "Jada?"

He heard sniffling coming from the closet. He gently slid open the closet and saw Jada sitting in the corner, crying her eyes out. Kalil dropped to his knees and began to rub Jada's hair. "Baby girl, what's the matter?"

"Nothing." Jada began to wipe her tears away as if she was okay.

It hurt Kalil's heart to see his baby girl in any kind of pain. He began to tremble. He gently grabbed Jada's face, making her look him directly in his eyes. "You would never lie to Daddy, would you?"

"N-no," she stammered, wiping her eyes with both hands.

"Why are you crying?" Kalil asked again in a soft tone. Jada didn't respond, but the look in her eyes immediately let him know that he really didn't want to hear the answer to the question. He gently grabbed her hand and asked her again, "Why are you crying, baby girl? You can tell Daddy anything."

"You pinky-swear you won't tell Mommy?" Jada held her fist up and extended her little finger.

"I pinky-swear." Kalil locked fingers with his daughter and kneeled next to her.

She dropped her head. "Fatboy tried to touch me again."

Kalil clenched his fist so tight, it began to hurt. "What?" he asked, his voice shaking. He felt like he was partly to blame if Jada had been harmed, because he'd left a void in her life when he was locked up.

"Fatboy . . . he touched me down there again." Jada pointed toward her pelvic area.

Kalil tightly clenched his jaws and gritted his teeth. His heart ached in a way it never had before. Jada had just delivered a crushing blow. He couldn't think of anything to say to her. Tears welled up in his eyes as he tried to be strong for his daughter, but the situation was too much to bear. A single tear slid down his cheek as he gently embraced Jada and rocked her back and forth.

"Baby girl," he whispered as he comforted his pride and joy, "it's okay. Everything's gonna be okay. Daddy will take care of you."

His sadness quickly transformed into complete rage as he envisioned Fatboy abusing his little girl. *He's dead. I'm-a dead that fat nigga,* Kalil thought as he cried with his daughter. He quickly wiped his tears away so that Jada didn't see him so weak. He picked her up and headed straight for the door. Then he went to the car and put her in. "Baby girl, stay in this car. No matter what you hear, don't get out, okay?"

"No, Daddy," she cried. "Don't leave!"

"I'm never leaving, Jada. I'll always be here for you. Now lock these doors. I'll be right back."

Jada did as she was instructed, and Kalil headed back into the house. He had some unfinished business. Kalil was so enraged, he was shaking uncontrollably. He couldn't believe that Destiny had allowed harm to come to their daughter. Staring at the world through rose-colored glasses, she didn't realize that Fatboy was sexually abusing her own daughter. Kalil felt that Destiny was just as responsible as Fatboy for the abuse, and they both would have to pay. At that moment, it was Destiny's turn.

Kalil stormed into the house, tears in his eyes and hate in his heart. He burst through the front door screaming, "Destiny!" He stormed into the back room, and Destiny was still asleep without a care in the world. He picked up the brass lamp that stood on her dresser and walked next to her. He held the lamp over his head, preparing to crush it on her head. "How could you?" Kalil said as he hovered over her. "How could you let him hurt my baby, Des?"

He couldn't bring himself to strike her with the lamp, so he dropped it and took off his leather belt.

Destiny felt the heavy leather belt wrap around her face and quickly jumped up. "Aghh!" she screamed, trying to figure out what was going on. The first thing she saw was Kalil's hateful eyes. Just the look alone would scare a person half to death.

Kalil, with all his might, struck her across the face again. *Whap!*

"Kalil, what the fuck is wrong with—"

Whap! He struck her across the back. *Whap!*

"Kalil! Stop it!" she screamed in agony.

"You let this nigga in here. You let this nigga touch on my daughter!" Kalil hit her again, this time catching her on the arm.

Destiny tried to block the hits, but they were coming too hard and fast. She balled up on the floor and tried to cover her face as Kalil swung wildly and nonstop.

Whap, whap, whap! The more he thought about Fatboy, the more he swung.

The thrashing went on for a good five minutes. He wanted her to feel Jada's pain. *Whap!* Destiny was balled up in fetal position and crying like a little child. Her screams registered in his brain, and he looked down over her body.

Kalil was breathing hard. He realized what he was doing and stopped swinging. He began to cry, saying, "Jada is coming with me. You're just as responsible as he is. Jada will never be with you. Never!" He looked down at Destiny and walked out the house to return to his daughter.

Destiny managed to pick her sore body off the floor to try to prevent Kalil from taking her daughter away. Her body had at least fifty belt marks on it. She had more stripes on her body than a zebra. She wasn't far behind him, yelling hysterically, "Where are you going with my daughter? Kalil! Kalil!"

She grabbed and pulled on Kalil's shirt, trying to stop him from leaving, but he pulled away from her and made it to the car. He jumped in the car and locked the doors while Destiny banged on the windows.

"Jada, unlock the door!" Destiny yelled as she stared at her daughter through the window.

Jada didn't even look at her mother. She looked over at her father and whispered, "Daddy, I want to go with you."

With that, Kalil pulled off, leaving Destiny screaming in the middle of the street. "I will never let anyone hurt you again, baby girl," Kalil promised as he placed his hand over his daughter's. The only thing on Kalil's mind at that point was to find Fatboy and make him pay for what he'd done. In his mind, Fatboy was already dead.

"You say this is his main spot, right?"

"Yep. This spot do about fifty a day. I used to trap in there before Fatboy took it over."

Kalil and Quinn sat outside of one of Fatboy's dope houses. They had watched over a hundred fiends come in and out of the house, but no workers. That told Kalil that Fatboy hadn't picked up his cash nor had it dropped off to him, and that there was a lot of money in the spot. They'd been there for the last four hours and saw no sign of Fatboy.

Quinn began to get impatient. "Yo, son, let's just run up in there and let his workers have it. Let's make him look for us. I'ma kill him for that foul shit!" Quinn cocked back his gun.

As badly as Kalil wanted to act on Quinn's idea, he knew it was too risky. He was willing to wait all night for Fatboy if he had to.

All of a sudden, Jada's situation became clearer. She'd told Kalil that she liked to dress as a boy because every time she wore dresses Fatboy would try to touch her.

"Nah, kid. It's the first of the month. He's eventually going to come and pick up his money, or one of his workers is going to lead us straight to him."

Just before Quinn could respond, a tall, dark-skinned guy walked out of the house with a black duffel bag in his hand.

"Yo, there go Duke. That's Fatboy's little man."

Quinn ducked down in his seat to avoid being seen. "Yo, let's follow him." He looked over at Kalil.

Kalil didn't even answer. He just pulled his hoodie over his head and yanked his pistol from his waist. Without hesitation, he jumped out the car and began to walk aimlessly toward the boy. Kalil's face was concealed under the dark hoodie and he acted as if he was drunk. Duke didn't even notice Kalil until he was about ten feet away.

"Yo, partna!" Kalil said as he stumbled on purpose, nearly falling.

Duke laughed at Kalil, not knowing that he was sober as a pastor. "Get yo' drunk ass away from me, son." He pushed Kalil away from him, causing him to fall.

In one swift motion, Kalil grabbed his banger, rose up, and pressed the gun to Duke's forehead. "Where the fuck is Fatboy?" he said through clenched teeth.

Duke dropped the duffel bag on the ground and threw both of his hands up. "Yo, I don't know."

"Oh, you think it's a game, huh?" Kalil looked Duke straight in the eyes. "Get yo' ass in the car." He grabbed Duke by the collar while still holding the pistol to his head. Then he picked up the duffle bag off the ground, pulled Duke to the ride where Quinn was waiting, and jumped in the backseat along with Duke. His trigger finger was itching. "Yo, I'ma ask you again—Where is Fatboy?"

"I don't know," Duke replied.

Kalil was tired of playing games with him. He pointed his gun toward Duke's thigh and pulled the trigger. *Boom!*

"Aghh! Aghh shit!" Duke grabbed his thigh in agony.

Quinn looked back at Duke and began to speak to him calmly, as if they were all friends. "My man ain't playing over there. If you know where Fatboy at, you betta spit it out."

"Or I'ma put another one in you. This time it's going to be in your face." Kalil put the pistol to Duke's head.

"Okay, okay!" Duke put both of his hands up between the gun and his head. "He went to VA this weekend. He goes up there to re-up once a month with his man. I swear, that's all I know," Duke said, tears forming in his eyes.

Kalil poked Duke in the forehead with his weapon. "When does he get back?"

"Sunday night," he said, holding his burning leg.

"Where is his spot?"

"He doesn't let niggas know where he stays, but he is always at his baby mama house."

"Where?"

"In Marcy. Nae-Nae stays in Marcy Projects," Duke said, his voice trembling.

Kalil opened the door and pushed Duke out, causing him to fall backward onto the curb. Kalil pointed his gun at Duke, but when he and Duke locked eyes, he couldn't bring himself to take him out.

Had it been four years ago, Kalil would've smoked him, but he just froze up. All he could see was Jada's face as he held the gun. He vowed not to leave her again.

Quinn noticed his cousin's hesitation and took matters into his own hands. He stuck his gun out his window and let off five rounds into Duke's body, leaving him dead in the streets and looking into the sky.

Chapter Five

The pounding sound of the rain hitting the roof awoke Kalil out of his sleep. He sat up on the couch, his perfectly toned chest, arms, and stomach stiff from the hard work that his new job required. "Damn," he mumbled as he arose and pulled his sagging pajama pants onto his waist. His entire body ached, and he was exhausted from staying up late all week. Every day after he got off of work, he and Quinn would camp out in Marcy Projects waiting to see any sign of Fatboy or his girl, but they came up empty.

"Fuck," he whispered as he rubbed his triceps. He knew that the heavy storm outside would shut down the construction zone for the day, and in a way he was relieved. He hated the fact that he had to work so hard just to eat.

"What up, bro? You good?" Quinn walked out of the bedroom and headed straight for the kitchen. He opened the refrigerator and examined the contents. He found a carton of orange juice and drank straight from it.

Kalil joined Quinn in the kitchen. "Shit, I'm hurting bad right now, bro. My pockets ain't as heavy as they used to be, and on top of that, I can't stop thinking about what happened to Jada. Fatboy pulled that foul shit, and all I can think about is deading his ass. These mu'fuckin' Italians got me on the clock too. I can't even concentrate on finding that fat nigga, because I got to keep this job. This gig is a part of the condition of my parole. This fucking construction shit is for the birds."

"That's because you trying to do something that ain't you, feel me?" Quinn stared across the table at Kalil with a serious expression. "You out here beating down doors to get legit, but that ain't you. The only way you know how to get money is the wrong way. That's just how we do. What you need to do is get in contact with Hova so we can get right again."

"I hear you, man," Kalil stated as he got up and left the table. There was so much temptation for him to get back in the game. He knew that if he got his hands on some work, he could flip a profit almost overnight. He kept reminding himself that he had one good reason to keep his hands clean, and that was Jada.

"Oh yeah, and you ain't got to worry about Fatboy coming around no time soon. Word out that you slumped his lil' worker and that you looking for him. He ain't gon' be showing his face no time soon, so Jada should be safe with Destiny until we get at his ass."

"That mu'fucka can hide all he want. He better enjoy his last days because I got something hot waiting on him when he does pop up." The news did ease his worries about letting Jada go back home to Destiny, however. He knew that he couldn't keep Jada away from Destiny for too long. All he needed was for her to call his P.O. and report the beating that he had given her and he would be sent back upstate without hesitation. He would take Jada back home, but he knew that Fatboy wasn't crazy enough to come around that way.

Later that day he got dressed and headed to Jada's school to pick her up from her dance class. He made sure that he was on time. He didn't want anybody picking Jada up but him. As he drove up to the school he thought about how he had yelled at Jada's dance teacher. He knew that he owed her teacher an apology for raising his voice at her the first time they had met. He also wanted to let her know that he would be the only person picking Jada up from now on.

He saw his daughter and a couple other little girls playing on the playground when he arrived.

Why are they outside in this weather? He walked over to pick her up.

Jada smiled when she recognized her father approaching and left her friends to run toward him. She splashed puddles of water with each step that she took, and the bottom of her pants was dark from being soaked in mud. "Daddy! What are you doing here?" she asked in a sweet tone.

"Why are you outside? Where is your teacher?"

"Ms. London told us that we could come outside to play. This mean man came in and was yelling at her, so she sent us out here."

"Okay, baby girl, go play with your friends for a minute. Don't leave this playground. I'll be right back."

Kalil walked into the building and headed for the auditorium. When he entered, he could hear someone crying behind the stage. He walked down the long aisle and made his way up the steps that led to the stage. "London?" he called out when he saw the fragile girl balled up in a corner.

She looked up and saw him staring sympathetically at her, and she immediately tried to wipe her eyes. Her hair was disheveled and she was shaking so badly that she could hardly stand. "I'm sorry," she sobbed as she attempted to rush past him. Her head was turned away from him and she was trying to stop herself from crying, but the tears were continuous. They would not stop descending down her face.

The sight of her made Kalil feel weak inside. The other day the young woman before him had been so confident and strong. Today she seemed to be a completely different person. He grabbed her arm lightly and turned her toward him. It wasn't until she faced him that he noticed her blackened eye. She also had blood on her face from her busted lip.

"Who did this to you?" he asked her. The look on her face revealed her embarrassment, reminding Kalil of a frightened child. He took her in his arms and rubbed her hair gently as he swayed back and forth.

"Jada is outside," she managed to utter as she avoided his question and pulled away from him.

"Ssh. I know where she is. I want to make sure you're okay," he told her, trying to help her regain composure.

London stopped trying to resist and finally cried uncontrollably into his chest. She didn't know why she was letting him hold her, but in a way it felt good. She felt safe in his arms.

"What happened to you?"

"He just came in here yelling. He grabbed me in front of the girls, so I sent them outside," she explained, her voice quivering.

"Who is he?" Kalil wished he'd been there twenty minutes earlier. He didn't know why, but he wanted to get his hands on whoever hurt her.

"My husband," she replied almost in a whisper.

Kalil lifted her left hand and noticed the large diamond that occupied her ring finger.

London tried to stop herself from crying, but the comfort of Kalil's embrace made her feel even more vulnerable.

"Here, sit down." He led her toward a chair. He didn't know exactly what to do for her, but he knew that he couldn't just leave her there. "Is there someone I can call for you? Do you need me to take you somewhere?"

London shook her head but didn't reply. She couldn't even look at him. The fact that he had found her in her current condition was humiliating. She always wanted to keep the fact that her husband was abusive out of the public eye. Usually when he hit her, he made sure that her bruises weren't visible. He would always leave his mark in places that clothing would cover, but this time he took it too far, interrupting her class because he thought that she'd lied about the times that she taught at the school. He was relentless in his attack against her and had left her with a black eye.

"I'm fine," she said through her tears. "Please just give me some privacy."

Her shaking body looked so fragile to Kalil, and he felt like he should do something. "I'll be right back," he told her as he got up and rushed to the restroom. He pulled paper towels from the dispenser and turned on the cold water. He soaked the towels in the water and then wrung them out. Then he rejoined London in the auditorium, where she sat still in the chair with her head in her knees.

Kalil made his way up the steps and knelt beside her as he lifted her head gently. "Here, let me see your lip," he said softly as he dabbed her face with the wet paper towels.

London looked toward the ceiling as Kalil removed the traces of blood from the corners of her lip. She grimaced when he touched her face.

"Ssh, I'm not gon' hurt you, ma," he said as he tried his best to clean her up. As he touched her face, he examined the beauty of the woman sitting before him. She was gorgeous, and he couldn't believe that any man would want to bring harm to her.

London finally looked Kalil in his eyes and was about to speak when they both heard the clanging of the auditorium doors as they opened.

Jada came running in. "Daddy, are you ready yet? Mommy gon' be mad if you take me home late."

London turned her head away from Jada. "I don't want her to see me like this," she stated softly. As Kalil never removed his hands from her face, London grabbed his hand with hers and hid behind it as Jada came near.

"Jada, go and wait in the hallway. I'll be right out. Just let me finish talking to Ms. London, okay?"

"Okay." Jada hesitated then let out a sigh.

"I'm sorry," London said, once Jada had left the room.

"Don't apologize. Are you okay?" Kalil rubbed the side of her face. He used a gentleness that he only shared with his daughter, and it made her force a smile.

She nodded her head. "I'll be fine, thank you."

Kalil reluctantly got up to leave. He didn't want to leave her alone, but he had to make sure that he got Jada home. He dropped his daughter off and then decided to call it a night.

Kalil couldn't get the thought of London out of his head. Every time he closed his eyes he saw her deep, dark brown eyes staring back at him. He knew that there was something about her that intrigued him, but he also knew that she was married. He wondered if she knew exactly how beautiful she was. Her smooth skin and exotic features were uncommon in the hood. Her perfect face looked like a creation of some famous painter.

He tossed and turned the entire night as thoughts of her raced through his mind. He was anxious for the morning to come, because he knew that he would get to see her again.

Chapter Six

The next day, after the storm had eased, Kalil went back to work for Mr. Moretti. Kalil wasn't the only black man that worked there, but they were all treated the same—like trash. It seemed like if you weren't full-blooded Italian, then Mr. Moretti had no respect for you. The only reason he even hired his black workers was because he knew that he could get away with paying them less money than advertised.

"Kelly!" one of the project managers yelled, calling Kalil by his last name, "go tell Mr. Moretti that we have another shipment coming in!"

Kalil was grateful for the break. He dropped what he was doing and went to relay the message. He walked into the room without knocking, but stopped dead in his tracks when he saw the pile of hundred-dollar bills on his boss's desk.

Mr. Moretti and the group of Italian men who stood around the desk immediately tried to cover up the pile of money.

"What the fuck is wrong with you? Are you fucking stupid or something? Close the fucking door!" Moretti slammed the door in Kalil's face.

Kalil quickly made his way back to his work area. *What the fuck they got going on up in this mu'fucka? This construction shit got to be a cover-up for something. It had to be about fifty stacks on that table,* Kalil thought as he continued to work. His mind was split between the money and Jada's dance teacher, and by the time his shift ended he was exhausted.

When Kalil got to Jada's school, she was the only student still waiting to be picked up. He stepped into the auditorium and smiled when he noticed that the stage lights were illuminated on his little girl. He smiled as he watched London instruct his daughter on her form. London held Jada's waist, and they dipped their hips in unison. Kalil clapped slowly as he climbed the steps to the stage.

"Daddy! Look what Ms. London taught me." Jada danced around the stage.

Kalil tried to focus on his daughter, but he couldn't keep his eyes off London. He could tell that she was embarrassed, because she refused to look his way. He approached her and stood silently as he waited for her to say something.

"Thank you for yesterday." She kept her eyes focused on the CD case that she had in her shaking hands.

Kalil lifted her face so that he could look her in the eye. "You good?"

London nodded. "Yes, I'm good."

"Did he hurt you when you went home?"

London looked at him. She didn't understand why he was so determined to help her out. "Why do you care?" she asked him, her brow wrinkled in confusion.

"I don't know. I just do."

He brushed her swoop bang out of her face and caressed her neck softly with his rough hands, sending goose bumps up and down her spine.

"Let me take you out?"

London raised an eyebrow. "Out?"

"Yeah, out. I want to get to know you." He noticed the skeptical look on her face and quickly added, "As friends, of course." He looked down at her, his stare warm and full of concern. He frowned because of the black eye. It seemed so out of place on her gorgeous face.

London couldn't help but stare back into his bedroom eyes. His lips were perfect, and she could imagine herself kissing him.

"I can't."

"Okay." Kalil nodded his head. He understood why she turned him down. He knew that she had a lot on her mind and that her situation wasn't as easy as his. She was married and, even worse, in an abusive relationship. Kalil would be patient. Her husband obviously didn't appreciate what he had. Kalil would wait until she was tired of being mistreated and would then show her how she deserved to be taken care of.

He touched the side of her face that was black and blue then leaned into her and whispered, "You deserve better."

With that he grabbed his daughter's hand and walked down the steps as he prepared to exit the room. Before he reached the door he heard her call his name.

"Kalil?"

He stopped walking and turned to face her. "Are you better?" she asked him, her shaky voice echoing through the large room.

"For you, I would be," he replied and then left the room.

From that day forward, Kalil made it a point to pick Jada up from school every day. He told himself that he was doing it for his baby girl, but truthfully a part of him wanted to check on London. He was attracted to her, and even though she was married, it didn't stop him from wanting to see her.

Every day he would watch as she taught her class. He told himself that he was there to show Jada his support, but he often found himself spending more time watching London than his daughter. He was infatuated by her style. Her smile was gorgeous, and when she danced, he saw a passion in her that was inspiring. Each day he would watch as London's bruises healed, but he always noticed when a new one would appear. He noticed everything about her, and he could tell that silently she liked the attention he was giving her.

"Why do you show up here every day?" she asked him one day as she gave the girls time to warm up by themselves.

"What? You don't want me to?" Kalil sat low in one of the auditorium seats.

London smiled and shook her head. "You have to stop this. I can't allow myself to start this with you," she stated seriously. Her voice was full of concern as she stood with one hand planted firmly on her hip. Her eyes watered over as she looked down at the man she desperately wanted to get to know. *Why does he have to be so damn charming?*

"Start what with me? I know you've got a lot to be afraid of. I would never put you out there like that. You're not doing anything wrong. I'm just here for Jada," he stated with a smile that melted London's defenses.

"I'm serious. You have to stop, Kalil. Just please don't complicate things for me more than they already are. You have no idea what I'm going through." London looked back at her class on the stage.

"I hear you, ma," Kalil stated as he stood up, "I hear you." He wasn't upset because he already knew why she was reluctant to fuck with him. She began to walk away, but Kalil reached for her arm.

"Oww!" She grimaced and quickly pulled her arm away.

Kalil turned her arm around and saw the red marks deeply embedded in her skin. Her arm was blotchy and swollen. Kalil shook his head in disgust. "You stay beautiful, a'ight. When you ready to leave that nigga, you let me know," he stated as he put on his fitted Yankees cap and exited the room.

London didn't know what to do. She couldn't keep her mind off Kalil. Even though she hardly knew him, there was something about him that kept her thoughts preoccupied. She couldn't help but think about the way he looked at her. His eyes seemed to penetrate her, and his presence made her heart race. *What the hell am I doing? I don't even know him,* she thought to herself each time she found her mind wandering off.

To keep herself busy she went to the school early to prepare for her class that evening. She loved volunteering at the performing arts elementary school. Her first love was ballet, but her husband never let her pursue her dreams. She figured that since she couldn't do it, she may as well teach other young girls how to. Now twenty-six, she'd wanted to join a dance company since she was a young girl.

She had been dancing since she was a five-year-old, but when she married her husband she was forced to give up all of her goals. She wasn't a dumb woman; she never had been and never would be. She was stuck in a bad situation and had no control over her own life.

Kalil had come out of nowhere, and she didn't know what to do with him. It was obvious that he didn't have much, but he had the swagger of a man who was working with big chips. She didn't know him very well at all, but the little bit of time that she'd already spent with him made her yearn for more.

She thought of him at night when she went to sleep, and he occupied her thoughts constantly throughout the day. She wondered what it would be like to be his. She knew that he had to have someone in his life, and she often found herself jealous of Jada's mother. What was she like? What made her so special? Why not me? These were questions she asked herself every time she saw him. She knew it was crazy, but she couldn't help herself.

She wanted to be a part of his life. *There's no point in starting something that I can't finish,* she thought to herself.

On the outside, her life appeared to be perfect, but on the inside she was dying slowly. She put in the Mary J. Blige CD, positioned herself in a dramatic starting pose, and waited for the music to begin as she got lost in her creative dance.

Kalil kept his distance from London for a while. He knew that she wasn't trying to leave her situation. It was evident that she was used to living the good life and he couldn't offer her that, so he stepped off. He kept his distance from her and kept his mind focused on providing for his daughter.

He worked day in and day out for Mr. Moretti, and the longer he worked there, the more he became convinced that there was more to the old man than what met the eye. Kalil was growing tired of getting fucked over by Moretti. He wasn't getting paid like he needed to, and his patience was growing thin. He was working like a slave, but still couldn't afford to cop his own crib and car. The only thing that he'd invested in was a new cell phone so that Jada would be able to reach him.

His cell phone rang, and he flipped the face up. "Hello?"

"Hi, Daddy," Jada greeted him, excitement in her voice.

The sound of his daughter's voice put a smile on his face. "Hey, baby girl. Daddy's at work right now. What's up?" He wiped the sweat from his brow.

"My recital is tonight. Are you coming to watch me dance? Mommy is coming. I want you to be there too."

"What time does it start?"

"At six o'clock."

Kalil pulled the phone away from his ear to view the time. It was already four-thirty, and he wasn't supposed to get off work until eight. *Fuck,* he thought to himself, knowing that he was going to have to leave early.

"Daddy, will you be there?" she repeated.

He could hear her getting teary at the thought of him not showing up. He sighed. "Yeah, I'll be there." He hung up the phone and went to Moretti's trailer to ask him for the rest of the day off.

Moretti never even looked up from his desk. "What the fuck do you want?"

"I need to leave early. I promised my daughter that I would be at her recital and—"

"Get your ass back to work before I fire you," Moretti said calmly. He still hadn't looked up at Kalil.

"What?" Kalil asked, feeling himself get heated.

"I don't give a fuck about your daughter. Get your ass back to work!"

Kalil nodded his head out of anger. He had to calm himself down before he did something to land him back in prison. He'd been disrespected by Moretti time and time again, but this was the straw that broke the camel's back. He decided to fall back and leave. *I'ma make sure this mu'fucka get what he got coming to him*. He took off his hard hat and threw it on the ground as he walked out of the office. He couldn't afford to just walk out on his job, but at the same time, he was a man and was tired of being degraded by Moretti. The only thing he wanted to do was be a good father and take care of his responsibilities, but it was almost impossible for him to do that in mainstream America. He only knew one way to get money and was trying to avoid that route at all costs.

He knew that Mr. Moretti would be upset with him for ditching work, but he left anyway. He had to be at Jada's recital, or he would never hear the end of it. He would much rather deal with the repercussions from his boss than disappoint his daughter, so when the shift manager wasn't paying attention, Kalil slipped out.

Kalil made sure that he stopped by the crib before he made his way to Jada's school. He knew that he would run into London and he wanted to be fresh when she saw him.

He walked into the full auditorium and made his way backstage. He found Jada standing in line with the rest of the girls, her long curly hair pulled up in a ponytail, and her pink ballerina skirt making her look like something out of a fairy tale.

"Daddy!" she yelled in excitement as she jumped into his arms. "Where's Uncle Quinn?" she asked, looking past his shoulders.

"He couldn't make it, sweetheart, but he told me to give you this." Kalil pulled a ten-dollar bill out of his pocket and handed it to her.

"That'll do," she said smartly.

"That'll do, huh?" he said as he tickled her. He hit her on the butt and told her to get back in line. He shook his head as he thought about how much she reminded him of Destiny.

London asked, "You ladies ready?" Then she wished them luck and sent them onto the stage.

When the lights in the entire auditorium dimmed, Kalil couldn't see anything but London's silhouette.

She could feel his eyes on her, and she smiled when she felt him walk up behind her.

"How you been, ma?" he whispered in her ear.

She kept her eyes on the stage as she replied, "I've been well. I haven't seen you in a while. You used to pick Jada up every day."

"What? You checking for me now?" Kalil was standing so close to her, his lips touched her ear every time he spoke.

She turned around and faced him with a slight smirk on her face. "Checking for you? How can I be interested in somebody I barely know?"

"Because you feeling the kid," he replied arrogantly.

The feeling of his breath bouncing on her neck gave her goose bumps and her nipples came alive. He placed his hands around her hips and pulled her close. His touch felt good and she wasn't going to stop him, even though she knew that she had no future with him.

She looked him up and down. He was clean in his light Sean John jeans and gray casual Sean John sweater. He wore a fitted NY cap that sat low over his eyes. He was looking good, she had to admit it.

"Let me get to know you," he whispered.

"I can't," she replied weakly. Her heart felt like it was going to beat out of her chest.

Kalil nodded his head and removed his hands from around her waist as he backed up. He knew there was no point in pursuing her; she was already taken. He wasn't trying to play games, and if she wasn't interested, he was going to step off.

"Is that an attitude that I'm sensing?" London joked as she noticed his change in mood. She looked back at the girls onstage to make sure that everything was going smoothly, but she quickly refocused her attention on him. She walked up on him and said, "It looks like you're the one checking for me."

"Something like that," Kalil replied, not masking his attraction.

London couldn't help but be intrigued by him. He was charming, and for some reason she could sense that he was sincere when he told her that he cared about what happened to her.

He put his hands on her neck and brought her face close to his. "You playing games, though."

"I'm not. You just putting me in a bad situation. It's not as easy as you think." She closed her eyes and pressed her forehead against Kalil's. "What do you want from me?" she asked.

He didn't answer her. He just kissed her lips lightly.

She opened her mouth reluctantly and pulled Kalil's lower lip into hers gently as their tongues were introduced for the first time. The tremor that London felt in her heart caused her knees to get weak. Their kiss would've become more intense, but the sound of applause caused them to snap back to reality.

London quickly broke their embrace and rushed onto the stage. She quickly thanked the audience for showing up and supporting her program. She then ushered her class off the stage.

The backstage quickly filled with parents coming to congratulate their children.

Jada ran up to her. "Ms. London, did you see me?"

"I did. You were perfect."

Kalil walked over and picked Jada up as he looked London in the eyes.

Jada put her hand in front of his face, trying to distract him. "Daddy, did you see me?"

"I saw you, baby girl. You did your thing out there," he commented.

His Brooklyn accent made London smile.

"Hey, baby girl!" Destiny shouted as she approached the threesome, her arms spread out for a hug. She was rocking knee-high Baby Phat boots and skintight jeans, and her wrists were cluttered with jewelry.

Jada ran up to her and wrapped her arms around her waist. "Hi, Ma. I did good, didn't I?"

"Yeah, my little mama was working it. You were the best dancer up there," Destiny replied. She immediately picked up on the tension between London and Kalil. She'd known Kalil for years and could tell when he was feeling somebody. The way he was staring at the other woman instantly made her jealous nature surface.

She stepped between him and London. "Hey, Kalil." She wrapped her arms around his waist and whispered, "I miss you," in his ear.

Kalil could smell her game from a mile away.

But before he could put Destiny in her place, London walked away, saying, "Excuse me, I need to go check on some of the other dancers."

"Yeah, you do that," Destiny stated smartly.

Kalil could see the expression on London's face as she walked off in a hurry.

He pushed Destiny off. "Don't do that."

"What you mean, don't do that? You all up in her face and shit. What, you fucking her or something, Kalil?"

"For one, don't be talking that shit to me in front of my daughter. Two, you are not my woman. What I do don't concern you anymore.

You fucked that up when you started fucking Fatboy."

"Why you holding on to old shit, Kalil? I'm sorry for fucking with Fatboy. You know that it's me and you. I'll drop his ass in a heartbeat if you tell me to."

Kalil shook his head as he looked down at her in disgust. "Take my daughter home. I'm not fucking with you, Destiny. Get that shit through your head," he spat out as he walked away in search of London.

The crowd had started to disperse, and he spotted her cleaning up the dressing room. "Yo, ma, I'm sorry about that. Jada's mother gets to acting up sometimes."

London didn't stop working. She walked around the room picking up after her students. "You don't owe me an explanation."

Kalil could see that she was upset. He reached out to her, but she dodged his touch. "London," he called out to her.

She finally stopped what she was doing to look at him. "What?"

"Don't be like this. That's Jada's mother. We're not together, so you don't have to be worried about her. That's just how she is."

Tears formed, but she quickly closed her eyes and willed them away. "Look, Kalil, it doesn't matter. You don't owe me an explanation. I'm not your woman, and I can never be your woman, so I don't have a right to be upset with you. She just reminded me that I can never really have you in my life. I messed up. I almost started to believe that I could be with you, but I can't. And it wouldn't be fair for me to expect you to be with only me when I can't guarantee you the same in return."

"I don't want a guarantee, London. I'm a man. I know what I'm getting myself into." Kalil touched the side of her face.

"No, you don't," she replied sadly. She removed his hand from her face and walked away, leaving him standing there alone.

Chapter Seven

London smiled when she saw the arrangement of lilies and baby's breath sitting on the edge of the stage. She looked around nervously and bit her bottom lip before plucking the card from the top of the bouquet to read the inscription: *London, I know you're in a complicated situation, but I can't get you off my mind. I'm feeling you and I want to get to know you, ma. Get at me anytime. (586) 638-4432.*

London quickly disposed of the flowers, tossing them into the trash. She wasn't trying to get caught up with Kalil. If her husband knew that he'd sent her flowers, there would be hell for her to pay.

It was easy for her to disregard the note, but when she received a new arrangement every day after that for two weeks, he became almost irresistible to her. She wasn't a fool, though. As quickly as the thought of him crept into her mind, she erased it. Her husband had a way of reading her thoughts, and she didn't want him to detect any trace of another man. She disposed of each and every bouquet that she received from Kalil.

But the more time passed, the more his sentimental gifts began to wear her down. *Get your shit together, London,* she told herself as she watched Jada and the rest of her dance class enter the auditorium.

Jada ran up to her and handed her a note. "Ms. London, my daddy told me to give you this."

London took the piece of paper out of her hand. "Thanks, sweetheart. Go and get changed for class." She opened the note: *Will you be my girlfriend? Circle Yes or No.* She burst out in laughter when she saw the words. He'd taken it back to the ol' school on her. *Oh, so he think he's cute.*

She folded the letter and put it in her purse. She was flattered by his persistence. He had simplified a situation that she thought was so complex. A part of her wished that she could get to know Kalil better, but she knew that it was impossible for her to ever get away from her husband.

As she taught her class that day, she tried to imagine herself on Kalil's arm. She wondered what it really felt like to be with someone who would genuinely care for her. Her head was on cloud nine as she tried to focus on the girls in her class. Each time she tried to concentrate on teaching them her mind drifted back to Kalil. He was charming, to say the least, and it was becoming harder and harder for her to say no to him.

She heard the doors in the back of the auditorium open and she turned to see Kalil walking in. He carried a single white rose in his hand. He was sexy in his baggy sweatpants and black Sean John hoodie. He approached slowly, as if he was tired, and he appeared to be carrying the weight of the world on his shoulders. His stress was apparent.

London instructed her class to keep practicing and she made her way off the stage toward him, wringing her fingers and looking around, even though she knew that there was no one else inside the room.

"So you checking *for me, huh?"* she asked as she approached him slowly. She couldn't stop the smile that blessed her face as he walked toward her. He looked good to her; in fact everything about him appealed to her. Even though she could tell that he didn't have much, there was something about his personality that attracted her. Money didn't matter to her. Her husband had money on top of money, but she was miserable

with him. Kalil seemed to be empty-handed, but the way he looked at her made her knees weak.

"You already know where my head at," he said as he stood in front of her. "You ready to stop playing games?" he asked as he handed her the flower.

London shook her head and stepped back to put some space between them, but Kalil stepped right with her, closing the gap.

"Stop. You can't do that."

"Can we talk somewhere . . . in private?"

"No, Kalil! I'm serious. You have to stop with the flowers and the notes. You can't do that. If my husband even thinks that—" Her words caught in her throat as she felt him massage her neck with his hand.

"You really want me to stop?" he whispered.

"You have to," she replied desperately. She could feel her heart beating rapidly. Fear, anxiety, and confusion caused her to tremble slightly.

"Can I take you out?" he asked.

She shook her head, but kept her eyes on the floor as she thought about what she wanted to do. *I can't do this. Just tell him no and stop this before it even starts.*

He lifted her chin. "Don't think about him when you're with me. You don't have to be afraid of him. The next time he touches you, I'm gon' put something hot in him."

A tear slid down her cheek, but she brushed it away quickly. *I can't.* "Kalil, you have to go. I can't do this with you. Please, you don't understand," she pleaded in a low whisper.

As Kalil stepped closer to her, she looked around frantically as if there were a million other people in the room. He noticed her hands begin to shake. "London," he started as he placed his hand on her neck. He could feel her pulse racing, and her chest heaved up and down quickly.

"You have to leave," she whispered.

"Look, ma, I'm feeling you. I just want to get to know you. If you don't want to fuck with me because you not interested, then I'll step off. But if it's your husband you worried about, that man doesn't concern me."

"He hurts me, Kalil."

It was the first time that London had confided in anyone. No one knew her secret, but now she had spoken the words and laid her cards out on the table.

"He hits me if he even thinks I've lied to him. He hits me. His punches are so hard that I can hear my bones bending when he connects. I can't—" Her words broke off in her throat.

He had no idea of the abuse that she encountered every day. "You don't have to worry about that. I won't let anything happen to you."

London nodded her head and wiped her eyes before she returned to the stage.

Kalil stayed and watched the two most important women in his life. He didn't understand why he felt so strongly for London, but he was feeling her tough and he didn't even really know her.

After class he dropped his daughter off at home and then took London to dinner. He stared at her across the table.

She wore large Chloe glasses to conceal her face and she was so nervous that she couldn't stop fidgeting. She blushed because she could feel him watching her. "What are you staring at?" she asked sweetly. She removed her glasses and peeked above the menu.

The sound of her accent was sexy and she had Kalil's full attention. The light from the candle danced on her dark brown eyes, as Kalil got lost in the specks of green that reflected from her eyes. "I'm just wondering how somebody like you got stuck with a nigga that mistreats you. You don't have to hide when you with me."

Embarrassment filled her face. "I know what you thinking, Kalil. I'm not stupid. You really want to know why I can't leave my marriage?" she asked as tears filled her eyes.

He didn't have a chance to respond.

"I have nowhere to go, Kalil. I don't have my own money. My father owed my husband a lot of money when I was younger. In order for him to pay off his debt he gave me to my husband. He took me away from my family. I was only sixteen when I was forced to marry him. The first time we had sex, his hand was wrapped so tight around my neck, I couldn't breathe. What can I do, Kalil? I can't go to the authorities. I have no identity, no green card, no visa, no Social Security card, nothing. He wouldn't even take me to apply for a license. He told me that he wants to make sure that there is no trace of me, just in case. He can make me disappear. You have no idea what it feels like to be me. I'm property. He owns me, and I have nowhere to go to feel safe. Do you know how it feels to not have anybody in this world? Yes, he hits me sometimes, but underneath it all, a part of him does love me."

"Love you? He blacking your eyes and you think he loves you?"

One tear slipped down her cheek. "I have to believe it. Every time he climbs on top of me, I have to believe something. If not, I feel worthless."

"I can't sit back and watch him hurt you like this."

"What do you want me to do?"

It hurt Kalil to his heart to hear her story. Just knowing what she had been through made him fall in love with her almost instantly.

He reached across the table and wiped the tears from her face. "I don't want you to do anything. Just let me make you happy. I know that I don't know everything about you, but I want to learn."

She got up from her seat and eased across the table so that she could sit directly next to him. She was afraid of what she was getting herself into, but at the same time she didn't care. She barely knew the man that sat in front of her, but she loved him. She didn't care what the consequences to her actions would be. She would rather live enormous than live dormant and was about to allow herself to be with Kalil.

He kissed her lips softly and passionately as she wrapped her arms around his neck. He could feel her heart beating wildly and he placed his hand on her heart to calm her down. "You don't have to be afraid with me," he promised. "I won't let anybody hurt you."

She looked into his eyes and knew that he meant what he said. Her feelings for him were so strong at that moment that they scared her. He was what her life had been missing. Kalil was the type of person that she wished she could be with. "I like the way that you make me feel," she admitted out loud.

Her words made his heart hurt because he knew that she would never be only his. He gripped the back of her head tightly. "Let's just take this slow. I don't want you to feel any pressure from me. I'm feeling you, so let's see where this will lead."

She nodded her head and smiled at him to lighten the mood. He didn't know it, but he had her entire heart in his hands and she was willing to risk everything she'd ever known just to be with him.

A waiter came over to their table and placed a menu in front of each of them. The waiter returned ready to take their orders after a few minutes.

Kalil flipped open the menu and observed the selections of the restaurant. He noticed that none of the meals cost less than $60. *Damn! These mu'fuckas taxing*. The construction job did not pay enough for him to be splurging on expensive meals. He knew that he couldn't afford the restaurant. Trying to impress London was going to break his pockets, but he knew that there was no way of getting out of it now. *Fuck it*. He looked at the waiter. "I'll take the lobster."

"I'll take the filet mignon with garlic potatoes," London said.

The waiter collected their menus and walked away.

"So tell me about you," London said. "You know about my situation and my life. Now I want to know more about you."

"There's not a whole lot to tell."

"Well, why am I just now meeting you? Jada's been in my class for over a year now. Why didn't you come around before?"

Kalil leaned back in the booth and debated whether he should tell her he'd been locked up. He didn't want her perception of him to change, but he decided he didn't want to keep any secrets from her. He wasn't the type of man to lie about what he had been through. He was born a hustler, and London would either have to accept all of him or nothing at all.

"Look, ma—"

"I told you about that *ma* stuff," she stated playfully.

He smiled at her. He loved the fact that she stood up to him. She didn't like to be called *ma*, which made him think that she didn't fall for game. She demanded his respect from jump, and he admired that about her. "All right, Miss London, I'm gon' keep it real with you because I don't want there to be any secrets between us. I did a bid upstate for four years. That's why you've never seen me around. I was getting money in Brooklyn when I got caught up, so I had to do a stretch upstate." He expected the news to scare her off, but the intimate look on her face never changed.

"So what do you do now?"

"Since I got out I've been trying to steer clear of the streets. Jada means the world to me, and I promised her that I wouldn't leave her again. I'm doing this construction thing right now, but that ain't really going anywhere. It's just another job. I work all day and don't make no real dough. That's how it got to be right now, though. I just got out and I'm not trying to get sent back upstate. I'm just trying to keep my head above water and be there for my daughter."

London knew that Kalil would never find a job in New York, at least not with a criminal record, but she respected him for staying out of the drug game for the sake of his daughter. "You really love your little girl, don't you?"

"Yeah, that's my shorty," he said, an instant smile gracing his masculine features.

"See, I want that. I want to feel that one day."

"What? You don't think that's gon' happen? Your husband doesn't want kids?"

"I don't want to have his kids. I want my children to grow up in a home. I want their father to be a great man. He's not that man."

Just then the waiter brought their food out.

By the end of dinner they felt like they had known each other for years, talking about everything, from their childhood to their life's dreams.

"So where does your man think you are tonight?"

"He's out of town on business for the next week."

When the waiter brought the bill to them Kalil opened it up. He already expected the bill to be high, but when he looked at the two-hundred-dollar tab, he knew there was no way he was paying for it. He looked underneath the table to see what type of shoes London had on.

"What are you doing?" she asked him.

"Making sure you got on the right kicks," he replied with a smirk.

"For what?" She frowned in confusion.

"Because we 'bout to dine and dash." He motioned for the waiter.

"Kalil, no!" she whispered, but a mischievous smile spread across her face. Her heart began to beat nervously as Kalil sent the waiter back to the kitchen for the dessert tray.

He got up and placed the white linen napkin on the table and casually strolled out of the restaurant.

"Kalil!" London whispered urgently as she watched him walk away. She looked back and saw the waiter coming out of the kitchen, so she finally got up and rushed out behind Kalil.

"Hey!"

She heard the waiter shout. She looked back and laughed when she saw the waiter fall onto the dessert cart as he tried to run after them. Kalil waited outside for her with his hand outstretched. She grabbed onto him as they ran up the block and out of sight of the restaurant. She could barely keep up with Kalil because she was laughing so hard.

"Oh my God!" she yelled as she finally stopped running and bent over in laughter.

He started laughing too and said, "Why you just sit there?"

"I didn't think you were really going to do it," she said in between her laughter. "I have never done that in my life. My husband would have never done that. That was crazy."

He grabbed her hand and pulled her near him. She let all of her inhibitions go as her body melted into his. She enjoyed being around him. He made her forget about all of her problems, and that night was the first time in a long time that she had felt truly happy.

"I better get you back to your car," Kalil said as he opened the passenger door to Quinn's car.

"I want to stay with you tonight."

"You sure?" he asked.

"Yeah, I'm sure," she replied and then stepped into the car.

Kalil pulled out and made his way to midtown Manhattan.

When they arrived at the hotel on Lexington and Fifty-first, London's heart felt like it would beat out of her chest. She was extremely nervous and her head was racing as she thought about what she was getting herself into. Her mind and her heart were telling her two different things.

Her mind told her to stop the affair before it began, to leave Kalil alone and never think about him again, but her heart told her that she was falling for him. The unfamiliar feelings felt so good to her that she didn't want to let them go.

"You okay?" Kalil asked her as he turned off the ignition.

"Yeah, I'm good," she replied.

Kalil could tell that she was nervous. The look in her eyes told him that she was unsure.

"Listen, when we go in here, nothing will happen that you don't want to happen. I'll never force you or pressure you to do anything that you don't feel comfortable doing, okay, ma?"

She nodded her head as she got out of the car and followed him into the hotel. She kept looking around nervously as if she would be caught by her husband at any moment.

Kalil grabbed her hand and led the way to the counter. Even though he couldn't afford to blow any money, he paid for the room, and they made their way to the twelfth floor. When they stepped onto the elevator, Kalil asked, "What you thinking about?"

"You," she replied with a flirtatious smile.

He turned toward her and pressed her body against the wall with his own. "Me, huh?" He slid his tongue into her mouth. His hands explored her body, the anticipation building in him as he rubbed her ass cheeks softly.

She kissed him intensely and grinded against his manhood as it rose to attention. She was hot, and her body was so aroused that she thought she would explode just from his touch.

When the elevator door opened, they broke their embrace and walked to their room.

London's body was tingling by the time they got inside, a feeling that was new to her. She had never been in a position where she was sexually attracted to a man. Forced into her marriage so young, she'd never experienced anything besides what her husband offered. She walked over to the bed and slowly removed her clothes piece by piece.

Kalil stood near the door and watched her undress. It had been a minute since he had made love to a woman, and his prison frustration was now apparent as his throbbing erection protruded from his jeans.

After London had removed every stitch of clothing, she crawled over to Kalil and stood up on her knees as she removed his jeans, releasing his ten inches. The sight of him made her pussy cream. She had never before felt the sensual, erotic sensations that were traveling through her body. His dick looked so good, she couldn't help but ask him, "Can I taste you?"

Kalil placed his hand lightly on her head and guided her mouth onto his shaft. His head fell back in pleasure as her warm mouth went to work. He got even more excited when he looked down at her as she massaged her throbbing clitoris while she sucked his dick. The only noise that could be heard was the flicking of London's tongue and the sounds of her moans as she took them into ecstasy. Kalil had never gotten head that good before and he couldn't help but to grind into her mouth.

He felt himself getting ready to explode, so he pulled out of her grasp before it was too late. He helped her to her feet and smacked her lightly on her perfect ass as they rubbed their bare bodies against each other. He led her to the bed, where he laid her down and spread her legs.

Her neatly shaven vagina gave him easy access to her clitoris, which he nibbled on gently, causing her body to tense up. She felt her wetness run down her legs as he introduced her to her very first orgasm. It was like someone was beating a drum inside her pussy, which contracted and throbbed until her body went numb.

"Kalil," she moaned to him. She was begging him to stop, but she wanted him to keep going at the same time.

He was biting down on her clit gently, causing her body to go crazy from pleasure. He knew his head game was nice. He wasn't like so many other men that were only out to please themselves. He wanted London to know what it felt like to be loved, sexually and emotionally. His soft tongue focused on her throbbing clitoris as he French-kissed her hidden jewel. He chuckled lightly to himself because the moans that London was releasing were unlike anything he'd ever heard.

She arched her back and locked her defined thighs around his head, trapping him in between her legs.

Kalil took his index finger and inserted it into her opening, fingering her as he painted her vaginal walls with his warm saliva.

"Oh my God!" London screamed as she gripped the back of his head and rotated her hips in a fluid motion.

One finger became two, and two turned to three as he finger-fucked her while munching on her with a passion that only a man that had been locked up could possess. His dick rock-hard, he thought that he would nut just from the taste of London. It had been so long since he'd been with a woman, he was more than ready to release his built-up tension.

"Kalil, wait, wait." London sat up and pulled his face up. "I want to feel you inside of me," she said.

He sat up, wiped her juices from his face and guided himself into her warmth. He thought that he would explode instantly. His dick was throbbing intensely from the feeling of being inside a woman again. "Damn," he whispered in her ear as he dug deeper and deeper into her. Every time he pumped in and out of her, his dick pressed on her clitoris, applying pressure to her pleasure zone. He took his time with her, and the feeling of her hands on his firm buttocks kept him aroused.

Kalil turned her around and placed her on all fours. He felt her body tense up, so he whispered in her ear, "Relax, ma. I won't hurt you."

London closed her eyes and gasped when he entered her from behind. She tried to run from the size of him, owing it to his size, but he slowly pulled her back onto his dick and kissed the nape of her neck each time he plunged into her wetness. He made love to her doggy-style and used a slow rhythm so that she would enjoy it too.

London stared in the mirror and began to massage one of her breasts. Watching their reflection and seeing the look of bliss on Kalil's face made her feel like she was in control. She bucked her ass back wildly as Kalil sped up his pace, hitting her G-spot again and again.

London pushed Kalil off of her so she could show him how she could ride his pony. As Kalil lay on his back, his pipe stood up like a leaning tower. The sight of his erect, slightly curved, throbbing penis made London lust for him even more. She gently straddled him and placed her feet flat on the bed. She then put him inside of her and slowly began to move in a circular motion, while going up and down.

Kalil's pubic hairs were completely soaked from London's love. And the only sounds that could be heard were their heavy breathing and the clapping sound that erupted every time her ass pleasurably slammed against his balls.

Kalil felt like he was in another world as he watched as London began to suck her own finger and stare deeply into his eyes. The connection was undeniable. He was experiencing the best sex of his life.

Kalil's rock-hard pipe felt so good to London's insides. It was so different from what she was used to. She had only been with one man—her husband—her entire life, and Kalil had him beat in size and stiffness. The experience almost brought tears to her eyes. Kalil gently rubbed her ass cheeks as she slowed down and began to grind on him.

London slowly took her hand from her mouth and placed it in Kalil's. Both of them were in complete ecstasy and totally in tune with one another's body. She began to circle her finger around Kalil's tongue. That was the final straw.

He couldn't contain himself anymore. He didn't even think to pull out before he exploded inside of her.

At the exact same moment, London gripped the sheets tightly as she felt herself cum for the second time, exploding on Kalil's pipe, her warm juices flowing onto his inner thighs.

Kalil turned London around and cleared her long hair from her face. The sight of her satisfied face was like a breath of fresh air for him. She made him feel good just from the way she stared back at him, and he silently wished that she didn't belong to another man. "You okay?" he asked as he stared into her eyes. He was looking for a look of remorse, but found none.

She laughed. "I'm okay. I don't know what I'm doing." She blushed as she covered her face with her hands. She was embarrassed and couldn't believe that she was here with him.

Kalil laughed, and when he smiled London admired his perfectly chiseled features. He laid his head on her stomach as she caressed the top of his head.

This is so perfect, she thought to herself.

She sat up on both of her elbows and looked down at Kalil. "Can we just stay here like this for the next seven days?" she asked him. "I just want to be near you. He's gone for the next week, and I want to spend every moment of that time with you."

"I can make that happen." Kalil wanted to say no. It wasn't that he didn't want to spend time with her, but he was going to have to spend a whole week's pay on the hotel room. He started to suggest something different, but when he looked up at her, he changed his mind. She was special to him and she was already unhappy in one relationship. He always wanted her to be pleased when she was with him, and he figured when her husband returned, their time would be limited.

He got up and slipped on his jeans.

"Where are you going?" she asked, a worried expression on her face.

He walked over to the edge of the bed and kissed her lightly on the lips. "To pay for six more nights."

The smile that spread across her face was worth way more than the cost of the room.

The next day Kalil woke up to find London still asleep. He reached over and pulled her close to him. He didn't want to wake her from her sleep, but he had to get to work. "Good morning, beautiful," he whispered in her ear.

"Mmm," she moaned drowsily. "Good morning. What time is it?" she asked, yawning.

"Six o'clock."

"I don't want to get up," she groaned.

They had been up all night, learning every single way to satisfy each other sexually, and her body ached in a good way. She didn't want to wake up to face reality.

"I know, ma. Tell me about it. I would like nothing more than to lay up with you all day, but I got to get Quinn's car back to him and get to work. I need to scoop Jada too. I take her to school most days."

London smiled as she rested her head on her hand. "You're such a good father, Kalil. I wish I had a father like you . . ." Her voice trailed off as she began to think of how her family abandoned her.

Kalil didn't know how to respond to her statement. He could see a sadness in her eyes, and he didn't know exactly how to take her pain away. After learning about her past, he understood why she allowed her husband to treat her the way he did. London was a beautiful person, but she had never been loved by anyone in her life. He pulled her close and held her for another half an hour before they finally got up to get dressed.

They rode back to Quinn's apartment, hands interlocked, as Kalil maneuvered through the city streets. They were both silent, but Kalil couldn't help but glance at her as she looked out of the passenger window.

He swung by Destiny's, and as soon as he pulled up to the curb, Jada came sprinting out of the house, her long, curly hair bouncing with each step that she took.

She paused in the middle of the yard when she saw her dance teacher sitting in the passenger side of her Uncle Quinn's car.

"Come on, baby girl," Kalil stated as he got out and picked her up.

"Daddy, is Ms. London your girlfriend?" she asked.

"London is Daddy's special friend. I care about her. You're supposed to care about your friends," he whispered in her ear and kissed her lightly on the cheek. He lifted his seat so that Jada could squeeze into the back.

"Good morning, Ms. London."

"Morning, Jada."

Jada stood up in the backseat and leaned over to whisper in London's ear. "My daddy likes you!" she said loudly and giggled.

London smiled and whispered back, "How do you know?"

Jada giggled. "Because he gets this dumb, goofy look on his face every time you are around."

London laughed out loud and then whispered back, "Well, I like him too."

When Kalil arrived at Quinn's apartment they all got out and walked inside. For some reason Jada clung to London, holding on to her hand as they walked into the building.

London felt uncomfortable and kept looking around constantly as if she were being followed.

"You good here. This is my hood," Kalil reassured her, and London nodded her head.

Kalil walked into Quinn's crib and found Quinn lounging on the couch with the remote in his hand.

Quinn's eyes immediately scanned London, and he nodded approvingly, but discreetly.

"Thanks for looking out, fam." Kalil slapped hands with his man and handed Quinn his keys in one swift motion.

"No doubt," he replied. He nodded toward London with a smirk on his face.

"Oh yeah, Quinn, this is London. London, this is my cousin, Quinn."

"Nice to meet you," London stated as they headed for the door.

Kalil put his hand on the small of her back and led her out of the room, while she held Jada's hand. He looked at his watch. "I've got to get to work."

"Jada can walk to the school with me," London said. "Will I see you today?"

"Yeah, ma. I'm with you as soon as I get off work. I can't afford to miss this money, but it's me and you every day after I get off work for the next six days."

She nodded as he kissed her softly on the lips and then bent down to kiss his daughter, who had a huge smile on her face. "What you smiling for, huh?" he asked as he tickled her. "I love you. Be good, okay?"

"Okay."

Kalil watched as London and Jada walked off hand in hand. He hated to admit it to himself, but London had captured his heart. The fact that Jada liked her made her even more special to him. He put his hand over his face and shook his head to get his mind right before he headed off to work.

Kalil and London were engrossed in each other for the next six days. The only time they parted was when he went to work. They satisfied each other completely in every way. Kalil was feeling London, and by the end of the week he knew that he would not be able to sleep a night without her next to him. He wanted her to be his. *She deserves to be mine,* he thought to himself as he watched her sleep soundly.

The next day would end their temporary escapade, and she would have to go home to her husband. Kalil lay down next to her and pulled her close.

She woke up out of her sleep and kissed him on the lips.

"I've been thinking, ma," he began, "I don't want you to go back home. I know we haven't spent a lot of time together, but I'm feeling you."

She looked him in the eye. "I'm feeling you too, Kalil."

"I want you to leave him. You don't even have to go back. We'll go get your shit tonight. London, you are my other half."

London sat up fully, and a tear slipped down her face. She wanted to leave more than anything. She wanted to be with Kalil. He'd made her feel things that she never thought she would feel—safe and loved. But it wasn't realistic for her to leave her husband. He would never let her go. "I can't," she whispered.

"Why can't you, London? You mean to tell me that this past week ain't meant shit to you?"

"You know it meant the world to me, Kalil. You mean the world to me," she cried, trying to convince him that her feelings were true.

"Then what's the holdup, London? Why won't you just leave him? If you're so unhappy, let me take care of you."

"I can't, Kalil. I don't have my own money. You are living with Quinn, baby. I can't come there with you. I'm stuck right now. If I leave him, where will I go?"

Kalil closed his eyes and shook his head in frustration. He knew she was right. He was down bad right now and he had to get his money up before asking her to be with him.

"What do you want me to do?" she cried almost hysterically.

Kalil held her and replied, "Nothing, ma. Don't worry about nothing. I'm gon' take care of everything. I'm going to take care of you. I'm gon' come up with some money, and then me, you, and Jada are going to be out, I promise." He held her as she cried in his arms. He was determined to come up with the cash to help her out. He wanted to be with her. He wanted to take care of his daughter. They were the two most important people in his life, and it was time for him to get back on his feet.

Kalil and London lay together and enjoyed the little time that they had left together before her husband came home.

Chapter Eight

London pulled her convertible Lexus SC into the driveway and made her way into her home. She had taken a shower before leaving the hotel, but she wanted to take another one before her husband returned home, not wanting to leave any signs that she'd been with another man. *I have a few hours before Jake is supposed to be home. I need to calm my nerves before he gets here,* she thought as she made her way to her bedroom.

She pulled off her sweatpants and T-shirt and stepped into her shower. Thoughts of Kalil filled her mind as she lathered her body. *Why can't I be with a man like him?* she thought as her own touch sent goose bumps down her spine. A smile spread across her face as she thought about the next time she would see him. He'd written his number down for her so that she would be able to contact him at all times, and she couldn't wait until the next time that she saw him.

She finished her shower and stepped out onto the cold tile floor. She noticed that her purse was lying on the bed with the contents spilling out onto the bedspread, and Kalil's number was in plain view. She quickly grabbed it and taped it underneath one of the dresser drawers.

Just as she placed the drawer back on track, a voice rang out behind her.

"Where have you been?"

London jumped at the sound of her husband's voice and the smile on her face was quickly replaced with a look of fear, as she attempted to discreetly close the drawer.

"Where the fuck have you been, London?" he repeated calmly as he sat back on the bed and awaited her response.

"Jake, you startled me. What are you doing home? I wasn't expecting you until later tonight. I was going to surprise you with dinner," she lied, attempting to change the subject and avoid answering his question.

"I caught an early flight home. I've been here since this morning. Now I'm going to ask you again—where have you been?" His tone became a bit harsher and he walked up to her and pinned her against the bedroom wall.

London's heart raced as she thought about the beating that was to come. "I just went out for a while. I wanted to find a good restaurant to buy dinner for tonight. I was lonely while you were away. I just stepped out to get some fresh air, that's all."

Jake snatched the towel from her body and wrapped one hand around her tiny throat as he forcefully shoved his other hand up her vagina.

"Oww! Jake, please . . . you're hurting me," she whispered as she tried to stand on her tiptoes to ease the pressure from his roaming fingers.

"Who were you with?" he asked as he probed her insides roughly. "I can tell you were with someone. My pussy feels different."

"Jake, please, I wasn't, I swear to you," she whispered.

His grip intensified around her neck as he purposely cut off her oxygen supply. He smiled as he watched her turn blue in the face. "You can't breathe, can you?" A demented smile spread across his face.

She clawed at his hand and kicked violently to get free from his hold, but he shoved her head against the wall and released her body, letting her crumple to the floor beneath his feet. She gasped for air gratefully as oxygen began to enter her lungs.

He looked at his hand, which was now covered in London's blood. "Go clean yourself up. I have a business meeting tonight," he barked as he left the room.

London cried so hard that no sound came out. She felt between her legs as blood leaked from her insides. Her womb hurt so badly that she could barely stand. She cringed in pain, closing her eyes and rocking back and forth. *What was I thinking? He's never going to let me go. He'll kill me before he sees me with another man. I'm trapped here.*

She lay on the floor for almost an hour before she finally gathered enough strength to move. She couldn't stop the river of tears that flowed from her eyes as she made her way into the bathroom.

Before she'd met Kalil, she would have never taken the beating from her husband so personally. But now that she knew what it felt like to be loved, she wanted more. She showered again and washed away the dried-up blood from her thighs. She let the water soothe the raw skin around her neck. *Why does he treat me like this?*

Just as she was about to turn off the water, the shower curtain opened and her husband stepped in with her. She cringed at the thought of what he might do to her.

"I'm sorry, London," he stated as he pressed his body against hers. "Why do you make me

hurt you like this? I just want you to be faithful."
He bent her over.

When she felt him enter her from behind, she said, "Jake, please don't. I don't think my body can take that right now."

He ignored her and began to pump in and out of her slowly with his long thickness. London bit down on her bottom lip to stop herself from crying out. It hurt badly from the damage that he'd done earlier, but she didn't want to give him a reason to harm her again, so she took it quietly and prayed for it to be over quickly. Silent tears stained her cheeks as she brought her husband to an orgasm.

When he was finished he smacked her ass lightly and kissed the back of her neck. "Get dressed," he told her. "We have somewhere to be in an hour."

London waited for him to leave the room so that she could scrub his scent off her body. She then stepped out and entered her bedroom. A long black Christian Dior dress was placed neatly on the bed with a set of four-karat chandelier diamond earrings and matching tennis bracelet on top. She dried her sore body and stepped into the dress. As she looked in the full-length mirror, even she had to admit that the dress was beautiful. It fit her body as if it had been custom-made just for her.

"I hope you like it," Jake said as he appeared in the doorway.

London continued to look in the mirror as she applied the jewelry. She'd grown accustomed to him buying her things, but she wanted love. And in her heart she knew that Jake could never give her that. To him, she was just a possession, another pretty thing that he owned. She was nothing more than his trophy wife. He wanted to have her on his arm in public, but in the privacy of their home he mistreated and abused her.

"Well, do you like it?" he asked again.

London couldn't believe he was acting so casually after just choking her out less than two hours ago. His personality was like night and day, and she was beginning to fear him more and more.

"Of course," she replied with a phony smile. "Thank you."

She applied a mineral powder to her face and neck to cover up the traces of their fight and then followed her husband out the door and into the limo that was waiting to take them to dinner.

London was in a daze as she sat at the dinner table. All she could think of was Kalil. She needed him, and she couldn't wait to get back to her dance class so that she could see him again.

"London, your dress is gorgeous. Is it Dior?" Tracy Reynolds asked.

Tracy Reynolds was the wife of one of Jake's potential business partners, and Jake had made it clear to London that she was to befriend her. "Friendly wives produce friendly business," he'd told her.

"London dear, don't be rude. Answer the question." Jake gave London a look that only she could interpret.

"I'm sorry, Tracy. I have so much on my mind. I was listening to the music and became lost in my own thoughts." London smiled graciously.

"Girl, tell me about it. These old love songs will make you think about how lucky we are to have these wonderful men in our lives."

London just nodded her head in agreement as her thoughts drifted back to Kalil. "Excuse me," she stated abruptly as she stood from the table.

Jake caught her by the wrist and yanked her indiscreetly, halting her from leaving.

"I'll be right back, honey. I'm just going to the ladies' room," she said and then walked away.

"I think I may join her," Tracy stated a minute later. "This will give you men time to discuss what you came here to discuss. Then maybe we can have some real fun and hit that dance floor."

London lifted her dress and sat on the toilet seat to find that she had blood in her panties. She knew it wasn't her period, which wasn't due for another three weeks. It must've been from the encounter she'd had with Jake earlier. She pulled toilet tissue from the roll and placed it in her panties. She didn't know why she was bleeding, and she hoped that Jake hadn't caused her any serious damage. Cramp-like pains began to shoot through her womb, and she doubled over in pain. *Oh my God, what's wrong with me?*

London got up and exited the stall. She hadn't stepped two feet before she was hit with another pain. She gripped the sink tightly as she held her stomach. Her insides ached, and all she really wanted to do was run and be with Kalil. She was definitely not in the mood to entertain Jake's friends.

Jake wanted her to be this beautiful prize for him to display for the world, bringing her to these dinners so that she could complement the deals that he brokered. He knew that she was eye candy and that every man that he flaunted her in front of would secretly wish that she belonged to them. She held her breath as another sharp pain shot through her abdomen.

Tracy opened the bathroom door. "London, are you okay?"

London immediately straightened up and erased the look of pain from her face. "I'm fine," she replied quickly as she turned on the faucet to wash her hands.

Tracy noticed that London couldn't keep her hands still. "Are you sure? You're shaking."

"I'm fine."

"London, you're not fine. What's wrong?"

London didn't answer her. She went into her purse and took her mineral powder out to apply more to her face and neck.

Tracy looked closer as she noticed what London was trying to hide. In the darkened atmosphere of the restaurant she couldn't see it, but in the brightly-lit bathroom she could clearly see the red bruises all over London's neck. She turned London's face toward her. "Who did that to you?"

"Nobody. I just break out in rashes sometimes. It's nothing," she said quickly. Her words stumbled out nervously, but confidently, as if she had rehearsed what to say if anyone asked her.

"London, that's not a rash, those are handprints. Did Jake do this to you? Does he hit you?" Tracy asked loudly.

"Aghh!" London said as another pain ripped through her petite frame.

"That's it. I'm going to get help."

"Wait, no! You can't!" London cried.

"No man has the right to hurt you like that," Tracy whispered.

"I know, I know. Please, Tracy, you can't tell anyone about this. Please promise me that you won't say anything."

"Okay, London, but if you ever need my help, you call me."

Tracy pulled out a piece of paper and wrote both her home and cell numbers down on it, and London took the number, knowing she would never use it.

Tracy helped London straighten herself up, and then they both walked back to the dinner table.

"What took you ladies so long?" Jake asked.

"I'm not feeling too well. I've been having these ridiculous migraines all day," Tracy lied.

London gave her an appreciative look as she took her seat next to Jake.

Tracy said to her husband, "Is it okay if we call it a night, sweetheart? I feel so exhausted."

"Sure. I think Jake and I just about handled everything that we came here to do. It was very nice to meet you, London." Mr. Reynolds grabbed London's hand and kissed it sweetly.

"The pleasure was all mine."

Tracy hugged London as if they were old friends and whispered into her ear, "Don't hesitate to use my number."

London was grateful for the kind words, but she knew that she would never call her. Her connection was too close to Jake, and he would kill her if he found out that she'd confided in one of his business partner's wives.

Jake and London rode in silence on their way home, until Jake's cell phone rang. He answered it, and London immediately sensed the mood change in the car. She looked over at Jake. His face turned cold, and his eyebrow dropped in anger as he listened to whatever news he was receiving from the anonymous caller.

"Of course, I understand," he stated in a short tone and abruptly ended the phone call.

"Is everything okay?"

"What is it?"

He yelled, "What did you tell Tracy Reynolds?"

"Nothing," she replied nervously. "I didn't tell her anything, I swear."

"You lying bitch!" He reached over her and opened the passenger door and tried to push her out of the car. "Get the fuck out of the car, bitch!"

"No, Jake, stop it! No! Please!" she screamed in fear as she watched the yellow line on the road pass her by at top speed. Her passenger door opened wildly as she tried to reach for it.

"Bitch, get out!" Jake was foaming at the mouth. "You want to tell my friends that I beat you? Huh?"

"No! Jake, I swear! Please . . . I love you! Plea-ease!" she sobbed uncontrollably as she struggled to keep her body inside of the vehicle. Luckily for her the car door slammed shut as Jake swerved to avoid a pothole.

When they reached their home, Jake got out of the car and literally pulled London out of her seat.

"Jake, please listen to me! I didn't!" she yelled, hoping that one of her neighbors would hear her. She knew that there was no one around to help her, since they lived in one of the most secluded suburbs of the city and most of the houses were at least a mile apart.

He pulled her to the back of the house and went into his shed to get a shovel and a flashlight.

"Jake, please don't hurt me," she begged.

He looked out on his many acres of land and pulled her into the thick trees that nestled behind their house. When they finally stopped walking, he handed her the shovel and said, "Dig!"

"What?" she asked through her tears.

He yelled, "Dig, bitch! Dig until I tell you to stop!"

London reluctantly began to scoop piles of dirt. She dug for what seemed like hours as Jake stood over her and watched. He had a look on his face that could only be described as devilish. *God, please don't let him hurt me,* she prayed as she continued to dig through the ground. Her arms burned unbearably and her tears clouded her vision, but she continued to dig because she was afraid of what would happen if she stopped.

Jake hopped down in the hole with London and grabbed her by the back of her neck as if she were a dog. "See what you drive me to, London? Huh?"

"I'm sorry," she replied through tears. She was horrified, quite sure that she'd just dug her own grave. *God, please,* she prayed. Beg for mercy, that's the only thing that she could think of doing.

"Are you trying to ruin me? You want to ruin my reputation?"

"No! I swear," she cried.

"Now it's your turn to decide if you want to live right and start being a good wife to me or if you want to leave. But this is your exit, London. This is your only way out . . . in this hole. What's it going to be, London?"

"I'll be a good wife, Jake, I will. I will be a good wife."

Those words seemed to snap Jake out of his rage. He pulled London close to him and whispered, "I know you will. Ssh, it's okay." He held her head close to his chest as she cried uncontrollably. "I love you, London. I wish you would stop making me hurt you."

She couldn't respond. All she felt was pain. Her body throbbed all over, and she could barely keep her eyes open as fatigue took over her body.

Jake picked her up and carried her back toward the house. He laid her down in the bed and kissed her on the cheek. "I love you," he stated. He waited for her reply, but was met with silence.

London sighed deeply and closed her eyes. She couldn't fight the exhaustion. She embraced the deep sleep as she thought of Kalil, hoping to see him again in her dreams.

Chapter Nine

The Lyfe Jennings debut CD lightly pumped out of the stereo as Kalil leaned back on the couch. His leg cocked and his eyes toward the ceiling, the lyrics had him in a daze. The song reminded him of London. He couldn't stop thinking of her and he hoped to hear from her soon. He'd just returned from walking Jada to school where he was hoping to catch London before her class began. When he didn't see her, he figured that he would catch up with her later.

Now he was trying to get his head together as he prepared to go to work. *I hate working for them rude-ass Italians*. Kalil took a deep breath, remembering how he dreaded working for someone else. His pride was bruised working for someone else. He had been a hustler as far back as he could remember. He had always been his own boss.

Now that he was taking instructions from another man it was difficult for him. He knew that he had to do what he had to do for Jada and himself, so he worked for peanuts and swallowed his pride. He was lucky that Moretti hadn't fired him for walking out on the job the night of Jada's recital.

The thoughts of returning to the streets invaded his mind constantly, but he stayed strong. He wasn't chancing going back to jail, and if he got caught hustling drugs, he was getting a one-way ticket straight back to Rikers Island. *This is all for Jada,* he thought as he finished up his breakfast and put on his steel-toe boots.

Quinn had stayed out all night so Kalil was going to have to take the subway to work. As he stepped foot on the New York pavement, he remembered back when he ran the streets. Even at eight AM there were corner boys hustling on the block, trying to get the morning crowd, which usually consisted of regular working citizens trying to get a fix to start their day off. Kalil smiled to himself as he watched grown men and women line up as if they were children in elementary school, just to get the monkey off of their back. "The early bird gets the worm," he said to himself as he walked past the crowd of addicts, repeating what he used to preach to his workers.

"Ayo, Kalil!" a man's voice said from amidst the crowd.

Kalil looked up and saw his lil' man, Peanut, distributing packets of heroin and taking money from the fiends.

Peanut focused his attention back on Kalil and smiled as he walked over to him, but some of the customers began to complain about not getting their packs quick enough. Peanut stopped dead in his tracks and turned toward the crowd. "Yo, shut the fuck up and wait for me. I know y'all see me trying to get at my mans right here. Keep complaining and I won't serve y'all shit. You can go uptown and cop some of that bullshit if you want to, if not y'all betta wait!" Peanut, shaking his head in disbelief, turned his back on them and faced Kalil. "Can't believe these mu'fuckas," he said in exasperation. "What's good, fam?" He extended his hand toward Kalil.

"I see you out here getting it." Kalil slapped hands with Peanut and released a slight grin.

"Yeah, the early bird gets the worm," Peanut said, repeating what Kalil had taught him years back.

"What's the deal?"

"Nothing much. I wanted to holla at you about something. This D.C. cat came through the hood yesterday looking for you and shit."

"Looking for me?" Kalil asked.

"Yeah. Dude was a stuntin'-ass nigga too. He had the new 6 Series joint with D.C. plates and all. He was flashing mad money too. He was giving niggas hundred-dollar bills to send the message to you." Peanut nodded his head.

Kalil's street instincts began to kick in as he received the information. He scanned the block and then looked back at Peanut.

Peanut noticed Kalil's uptightness and then spoke up. "Nah, Kalil, he wasn't on no beef shit. He said you two were good friends and he needed to link back up with you. I think he said his name was"—Peanut stopped mid-sentence, trying to remember the man's name. He looked down and began to rub his goatee in an effort to jog his memory—"June! Yeah, his name was June. He left a number for you," Peanut said as he took out his cell phone and flipped it open.

When Kalil heard June's name, he instantly knew who it was. June was his former cell mate in Rikers Island. *June must've gotten out and is trying to do business. I guess he was serious. It would be good to see that crazy mu'fucka again,* Kalil thought.

A wave of relief overcame him. The mention of someone looking for him had him uneasy. He knew he had accumulated a lot of enemies by being in the streets all his life and quickly grew defensive.

He looked at Peanut's phone. "What's the number?"

As Peanut recited the numbers, Kalil made a mental note of it. He had a sharp memory and planned on giving June a call later. "Yo, I got to bounce. I'ma catch up with you later." Kalil slapped Peanut's hand.

Peanut looked Kalil up and down and noticed his steel-toe boots and his work gloves that hung out his back pocket. He then looked at Kalil's lunch pail. He never knew Kalil to be a nine-to-five type of person, just a bona fide hustler. He used to look up to Kalil and wanted to be just like him. While other kids wanted to be a fireman or a lawyer, Peanut wanted to be just like Kalil the dopeman. He used to see how much people respected Kalil, and Peanut admired the street fame. He couldn't believe that Kalil was punching in on a clock.

"I see you laying low for a minute. Those folks got you on paper, huh?" Peanut said, referring to Kalil being on probation. He looked Kalil square in the eye. "When you get back in, I want to get down."

Kalil knew that Peanut would be a trustworthy soldier. The gesture meant a lot to him. He knew that Peanut was one of Hova's disciples and knowing that Peanut was ready and willing to leave that team was a display of pure loyalty, but he knew that he couldn't take Peanut up on his offer. He was out of the game for good.

"I can't mess with the game anymore. I'ma catch up with you later though, lil' man."

Just before Peanut could respond, something gained all of Kalil's attention, causing him to look away from Peanut. An all-black Benz slowly crept up the block, with FATBOY on the plates. Fatboy had his window down and was so busy bobbing his head to his music, he didn't notice Kalil. Kalil's heartbeat sped up, and he involuntarily began to grit his teeth and clench his fist.

Peanut noticed the sudden change in Kalil's mood and followed his eyes to see Fatboy's Benz park down the block. "I never liked that fat mu'fucka either," Peanut said as he remembered back when Kalil used to tell him how grimy Fatboy was and not to associate with him. "He fucks with the chick that stay right there." Peanut threw his head in the direction of the house Fatboy was parked in front of.

Kalil watched as Fatboy got out the car and scanned the block. Kalil dropped his head, hoping Fatboy didn't notice him. Obviously Fatboy didn't see him, because he hit his car alarm and proceeded to the house.

Kalil talked through his clenched teeth. "You got the banger on you?"

"You know it!" Peanut pulled out his black .45 pistol out of his waist and handed it to Kalil.

Kalil looked at the gun in his hand and realized that it had been four years since the last time he had gripped a banger. He didn't want to admit it, but it felt damn good to him. The images of Jada crying and balled up in the corner of her closet kept popping into his head. Rage quickly filled his heart and he was ready to put his murder game down. Soon after, the images of him sitting in a jail cell and Jada growing up without a father emerged. He wanted to get at Fatboy so badly. He was so close to revenge, he could taste it.

Kalil gave Peanut the gun back and whispered to himself, "I can't do this . . . I can't." And he headed toward the subway. That was one of the hardest things he'd ever had to do—walk away.

"Oooh! Right there, Fatboy," the young girl said as Fatboy's face was buried into her crotch. Her legs were straight up in the air as Fatboy alternated between licking her clitoris and asshole. Fatboy was a certified freak and nothing was off-limits for him. He went the majority of his life being laughed at and teased for his weight and never got any play from the ladies, so when he began to make a little bit of money, he used it to his full advantage. His newfound street fame attained him instant popularity with the ladies, and he had a reputation for tricking off his money, causing all the local hood rats and sack-chasers to check for him. Fatboy's motto was "It ain't trickin' if you got it," and he definitely did have it. Fatboy was moving heavy weight within the city and was the only successful drug dealer in the area, besides Hova's disciples.

"Come here, ma." Fatboy flipped over onto his back totally naked and held his dick firmly as he began to stroke it. The young girl began to straddle Fatboy and he guided her love box directly onto his lips. Fatboy used his tornado tongue and went to work. She rode his tongue as if it was his pipe, moving her body in wild circular motions. Fatboy's dick was now standing at full attention and he was ready to lay it down.

He forcefully pushed her off of his face, so hard that she plopped down on his fat belly. He picked her up and dropped her square on his pole. She began to ride him passionately as sweat dripped off of her body.

The girl closed her eyes and pretended that she was sexing someone else besides Fatboy. She was totally disgusted by his sloppy appearance, but he paid to play and she was about her money.

Fifteen minutes later Fatboy was putting on his pants and leaving the girl with semen all on her face. He finished getting dressed and admired the girl's perfect frame and pretty face. He peeled off five crispy hundred-dollar bills, tossed it on her bed without saying a word, and walked out feeling rejuvenated.

As Fatboy walked out the door he saw Peanut leaning on his car, his arms crossed, as if he was waiting on him.

"What the fuck is you doing, lil' nigga?" Fatboy yelled. He put his hand under his shirt and gripped his pistol. He remembered Peanut from the block and knew that he was once Kalil's lil' man.

"Nah, it ain't like that." Peanut lifted up his shirt to show Fatboy he wasn't on any beef tip. "I just want to holla at you, Fatboy."

Fatboy was still cautious and kept his hand on his banger as he walked over to Peanut. "What you got to holla at me about? I don't rock with you like that."

"Look, man, I'm trying to get down, man. I see you out here getting it and all." Peanut turned back and looked at Fatboy's new Benz.

"Nah, son, I roll by myself. If you knew what was best for you, you would get the fuck off of my whip." Fatboy walked up on Peanut.

Peanut stepped to the side and let Fatboy get into his car. He tried explaining to Fatboy that he was trying to give him some valuable information and not trying any funny business. He stood outside's Fatboy's window and tried to put him up on game before he could speed off.

"Yo, Kalil was asking about you," Peanut blurted out, gaining Fatboy's full attention.

"Is that right?" Fatboy checked his rearview mirror. He knew that the next time he saw Kalil it was going to be trouble. He knew that what he did to Jada would cause any father to want to kill. He wasn't going to get caught slipping. He rested his hand on his chrome .38 handgun that he had on his lap.

"Yeah, but that bitch-ass nigga is gone already," Peanut said with anger in his eyes.

Fatboy examined Peanut and knew that he had ill feelings toward Kalil, from his facial expression. "I thought that was yo' man?" Fatboy gripped his pistol, being extra cautious.

"Yeah, he was, but since he's been out, he's been acting funny. He ain't the same dude anymore. I don't respect that man like I used to. So what up? Can we talk business?"

Fatboy checked his mirrors again and then looked back at Peanut. He knew Peanut was sincere. "What business you talking about?"

Peanut smiled, knowing that Fatboy was willing to listen. "I got this cat from out of town that wants some major weight, and I need a plug on them thangs," he said, referring to bricks of cocaine. He approached Fatboy's car.

"I thought you worked for Hova. Why don't you holla at him? I know he got them shits by the boatload," Fatboy said.

"Yeah, but I'm trying to do my own thing. I need a new source, nah mean? Hova try to stay in a nigga pocket. I don't want him to know all my moves," Peanut explained to Fatboy, moving his hands to emphasize his point.

Fatboy could relate to Peanut. He knew how it felt when you were ready to become your own man and make your own moves. Fatboy put his pistol under his seat. Knowing that Peanut was serious, he was ready to talk business. He asked, " 'Bout how many he say he wanted?"

"Like ten of them," Peanut said confidently.

Fatboy hit his *unlock* button. "Get in. Let's talk business."

Peanut got in the car and started explaining the situation to Fatboy, and Fatboy, so eager to get some money, was all in.

Fatboy and Peanut sat in the same spot for thirty minutes talking about their new partnership. Fatboy had lit up two blunts with Peanut as they sat there and talked.

"Yo, I didn't know you were cool like this, nah mean?" Fatboy passed the Dutch over to Peanut.

"Yeah, I'm a real nigga. Kalil had me thinking you were a lame. You cool too." Peanut hit the Dutch and inhaled deeply.

"Yeah, man. I think we can really make some money together, man." Fatboy reached out his hand and slapped palms with Peanut.

"Yo, man, look in my eyes, fam," Peanut said with a serious face. "I've been dying to tell you something."

"What's that?" Fatboy asked as the weed took its effect on him.

"Surprise," he said in a low tone.

Just then Fatboy felt cold steel pressed to the back of his head. It was Kalil standing outside of his driver's-side door. Fatboy's heart dropped as he realized he had been set up.

Peanut smiled as he saw the instant change in Fatboy's face. He then spat in Fatboy's face when he thought about what he'd done to Kalil's little girl. After Kalil had told him what Fatboy had done, Peanut was down for whatever. He hopped out the car and looked over at Kalil pressing his gun to Fatboy's head.

"Thanks, lil' man," Kalil said through his clenched teeth.

"No doubt. I had to pretend I liked that fat fuck!" Peanut walked over to Kalil and prepared to get in the front seat.

Kalil couldn't fathom the thought of letting Fatboy get away. Fucking his chick was one thing, but he had crossed the line when he had touched Jada. So he turned back around and devised a plan to catch Fatboy slipping, and it worked like a charm.

Kalil focused his attention on Fatboy and struck him across the face with his gun. "Move over, bitch-ass nigga!" Kalil grabbed Fatboy's collar and shoved him over to the passenger-side seat.

With his gun still pointed at Fatboy, he slid in and sat directly behind him, and Peanut slid into the driver's side and pulled off.

Kalil wanted to blow Fatboy's brains out right then, but he remained patient. Almost.

Whack! Whack! He hit Fatboy in the back of his head with the butt of the gun, causing blood to gush out.

"Fuck!" Fatboy screamed as he held the back of his head. Blood trickled down his fingers and onto his all-white interior. "Yo, chill, man. I'm sorry, man!" Fatboy said as he came to the realization of life coming to an end.

"How could you touch my daughter? How?" Kalil yelled. He reached around and punched Fatboy on the brim of his nose.

"Aghh!" Fatboy grabbed his nose. All the wrong he had done began to eat at his conscience. He knew that touching on Jada was wrong, but he couldn't help it. His uncontrollable urge got the better of him.

Tears formed in Kalil's eyes as he thought about his daughter and how her innocence was stripped away by the fat bastard that sat in front of him. He wanted to send the hollow-tip bullet directly into the back of Fatboy's head, but he had to wait until Peanut pulled up to a low-key spot.

Kalil choked Fatboy from behind and whispered in his ear, "Today you meet yo' maker."

"I'm sorry. I'm sorry," Fatboy managed to squeal out as Kalil cut off his oxygen supply.

Peanut pulled up to Central Park, where the morning joggers were doing their daily workout. He put the car in park and watched as Fatboy began to slip out of consciousness from Kalil choking him. He waited for the joggers to pass by and began to wipe down the door handles on the car. He didn't want Kalil's or his fingerprints to be left behind. He then jumped out of the car and into Quinn's, who was waiting for them there.

Kalil had everything mapped out and had called Quinn to tell him that he knew where Fatboy was. Quinn immediately jumped out of bed with his one-night stand and hurried over.

"Yo, Kalil, I—"

Boom!

A single shot rang out before Fatboy could even finish his sentence. Kalil had let off a slug into the back of his dome, splattering his brains on the front dash and windows. The front window appeared as if it had red tint, because of all of the blood.

Fatboy's lifeless body slumped in the seat. Kalil slid out the driver's-side door and into Quinn's car, his adrenaline pumping as he stared at the bloodstained window and at Fatboy's dead body. A sense of redemption overcame him as he rested his head on Quinn's headrest.

Peanut passed him his bandanna, and Kalil wiped off the murder weapon and tossed it out the window. And a huge burden was lifted off of Kalil's heart as Quinn pulled off.

Kalil hopped out of Quinn's car and walked over to the construction site. He was an hour late for work and knew that his boss would be angry with him. *What can I tell this mu'fucka?* Kalil asked himself as he walked onto the site.

"Yo, Kareem, or whatever your fucking name is, you're late!" his boss said as he was loading a truck with cement bricks.

"I know. I can explain though. My—"

"I don't give a fuck why you're late. Drop off your fucking hard hat and get the fuck off my property. You're fired!" he yelled, not even bothering to look at Kalil.

"Wait, I really need this job. I had an emergency." Kalil followed his boss around, trying to get him to talk to him.

"You're fired! I do not need anyone slowing us down. Time is money, *brutha*," the Italian said as he brushed past Kalil.

Kalil got the picture and threw his hard hat at the man and walked off. *Fuck this shit, man! I don't need this. I ain't cut out for this. I'm a hustler, and that's what I do!* Kalil's mind began to race. He knew that he'd made a bad judgment call by going after Fatboy and causing himself to be late. But he had to handle the situation with Fatboy. For Jada.

Kalil headed to the subway and headed home. He had a phone call to make. He was about to get back in the game, where he'd be his own boss. The thought of June popped in his head, and he knew that he would be trying to make some moves. Kalil was about to get on his hustle.

Chapter Ten

"Okay, you are all set, young lady. You will be sore for a few days, but you should be fine." The doctor walked over to Jake and shook his hand.

"Thanks for coming through, Doc. If she needs you, I will give you a call."

The doctor left the room, and fear took over London's body as Jake stood over her.

"I'm sorry, London. I just get so angry all the time. I do love you, though. I don't want to lose you."

"I love you too," she responded, afraid that he would harm her.

"Do you need anything?"

It was obvious that he was feeling guilty about the way he had acted the night before and he was trying hard to make things up to her.

"I just need to get to the dance school," she told him as she attempted to get up.

"That can wait for a couple days. You need to rest. In a few days you can go back. I have a surprise for you." Jake pulled out a small box.

London already knew what it was. Jake would always shower her with expensive gifts after he would beat her. He opened the box and displayed the five-karat diamond cross that hung on a thin platinum chain.

"Thank you, Jake," London said, a phony smile plastered on her face. She grimaced because of her swollen jaw, but tried her hardest to hide her discomfort.

London turned on her side as a tear ran down her cheek. She needed to see Kalil. She had to see him. He was the only person who made her feel safe. *After last night, I don't know what he is capable of. That is the worst that it has ever been, and I'm not willing to risk my life by being with him anymore. The first chance I get, I am leaving. I can wait a couple days, but when I do get out of this house, I'm never coming back.*

Days passed and London still hadn't gotten the chance to speak with Kalil. She hadn't been able to contact him since the day she last saw him. Her husband had been extra suspicious of her. Things between her and Jake only worsened. He had told her that he had to keep her trained, and it seemed as though the beatings came more often and without provocation. The blows that he inflicted on her left bruises that were deep red, and it hurt her badly to even touch them. The physical abuse had become too much for her to bear. She was broken mentally, spiritually, and physically. The only thing that kept her sane was the thought of Kalil.

She swore that as soon as she got the chance to call him that she would leave with him.

Jake controlled every aspect of her life. He didn't allow her to have her own bank account, so she had no money. She didn't have any family in the States, so Jake was her only family. She felt like a slave in her own skin, and it was breaking her down. The only time Jake let her leave the house was to teach dance, and the only reason he agreed to that was because he beat her unconscious one time and that was his way of apologizing.

She was tired of living her life in fear and she desperately wanted out. She hadn't been allowed out of the house, and when her husband wasn't home he locked all of the doors and windows with a key that only he possessed. She felt like a prisoner in her own home. She was like a dog that Jake had trained to fear him.

London searched frantically for the piece of paper with Kalil's phone number. Her hands shook uncontrollably as she pulled her panty drawer from the dresser and looked underneath, where she had it safely taped. *Oh my God, it's not here. I know I put it here,* she thought to herself as she got on her hands and knees to make sure that the paper hadn't fallen to the floor. *Where is it? I have to get out of here,* she thought as tears began to surface and flow freely.

She tore her room up looking for Kalil's telephone number, but she knew that she had only hidden it in one place. *He found it. Oh my God, he found it,* she thought as tears of trepidation seized her.

She needed Kalil now more than ever. All she wanted to do was be with him. He had shown her a happiness that she had never felt before and she yearned to feel that way again with him. She didn't know how or when, but the first opportunity she got to run away, she was going to take it.

Kalil was eager to get in contact with June. He had called him a couple days ago to see if he was trying to do business, but he had gotten his voice mail. He was awaiting the return phone call. He knew that business with June was going to put him back on top, where he was supposed to be.

"Yo, you sure you know this nigga?" Quinn looked at his cousin with a serious expression on his face.

Kalil sensed a little bit of jealously from Quinn. He knew that Quinn wouldn't be too fond of the fact that he was doing business with someone other than him. "Yeah, from what I know, my man is good. Besides, this is a one time flip. One last run and I'm out," he explained.

I've been asking this mu'fucka to get back in the game since he got out, and he been telling me no. Now he jumping at the opportunity to do business with this D.C. cat, Quinn thought silently. There was a bit of jealousy in his heart, but he wasn't going to stop Kalil's hustle. That was his family, and he knew that he was doing what he had to do.

"Let me know if you need to put me on."

"I think I'm gon' do this one solo, fam, but you know I'm gon' look out for you afterward. You been holding me down since I got out the joint. You ain't showed me shade even once, and you welcomed me to your car, crib, clothes, whatever I needed to get by. I appreciate that, and I'm gon' look out for you. This is about to be both of our paydays, trust me."

"It's about time you took your throne back anyway, show these niggas who the king of New York is."

"Nah, man, it ain't even like that. I'm doing this so that I can blow this fucking city. As soon as I get off parole, I'm gon' take Jada and London and get out of here."

"London? Damn, cuz, you feeling ol' girl like that? Didn't you say chick was married?"

"Yeah, man, but I'm feeling shorty, and her situation ain't what you think it is. She a different type of woman. She with me even though I ain't got shit to offer her. When I'm with her, she makes me feel like a man . . . her man, like she's proud to be with me, son."

Quinn smirked and shook his head from side to side. "Damn, she got you out here caking it," he joked.

"Nah, fam, it ain't like that. She just built for me, and Jada love her, so I can't lose. I just got to get this money so I can take care of my daughter and her."

"I hear you, yo."

Kalil knew that the type of money he was about to come into could change his life for the better. He definitely planned on investing in a business so that he could flip his money the legal way, and he wanted to start a family with London and provide Jada with the best of everything that money could buy. All he needed was for June to hit him back so that he could get the ball rolling.

He decided to go and pick up his daughter. He hadn't discussed his plans of taking Jada away with Destiny, and he knew that he would need her permission before he did. He took the 6 train to 125th and walked the remaining distance to Destiny's home in Harlem. He told himself to be cool when he saw his baby mama. He still hadn't forgiven her for what she had allowed to go down with Fatboy.

He got out the car and walked into Destiny's house. He didn't bother to knock, since he was the one who had purchased it for her in the first place.

Kalil snuck up on Jada, who was in the kitchen standing on top of one of the dining chairs, trying to reach for something on top of the refrigerator, and scooped her in his arms. "Boo!" he shouted loudly as he picked her up and lifted her above his shoulders.

"Daddy! You scared me," she said as she held onto the top of his head.

He put her down. "Where's your moms?"

"She in her bedroom," Jada responded as she climbed back onto the chair.

Kalil patted her lightly on the bottom. "Get down before you hurt yourself. What you reaching for, anyway?"

"The Fruity Pebbles. I'm hungry."

Kalil grabbed the box of cereal off the top of the refrigerator and set it on the countertop. He then opened the refrigerator door and pulled out a gallon of milk. He checked the date and noticed that it was expired. He looked to see what else Destiny had to eat, but the refrigerator was bare. "You ain't eaten all day?" he asked his daughter.

She shook her head no.

I'm gon' fuck Destiny's ass up. Fuck is wrong with her? "Go watch cartoons, baby girl. I'll take you out to eat in a minute."

He walked down the hallway and found Destiny's room door slightly cracked, her room trashed. Kalil had to hold his breath just to stop himself from gagging at the funky scent of stank pussy and dirty laundry. He'd never known Destiny to be trifling. She had definitely changed since the days that she was his wifey.

"Des, wake up." Kalil tapped her shoulder. He pulled back the covers, and what he saw hurt his heart. Destiny's badly burned lips were still wrapped around the blackened crack pipe that she gripped in her hand.

His heart dropped to his stomach as he sat down on Destiny's bed. He hadn't even noticed that she had developed a crack habit. *How the fuck did I miss this?* Even though they weren't together, he still didn't want to see her like this.

"Des, baby, wake up." Kalil lifted her head and rested it in his lap. He felt as if somehow this was his fault. *I should've been here for her,* he thought as he watched her stir out of her sleep.

She opened her eyes and sat up frantically when she saw Kalil looking down at her. She immediately jumped out of bed and started swinging. "Don't touch my baby! You sick bastard! Why'd you touch my daughter?"

"Destiny, chill out!" Kalil screamed as he grabbed her and bear-hugged her tightly to prevent her from swinging at him.

"Fatboy, why'd you touch my daughter? I should kill you, you fat, nasty bastard!" she screamed as she cried frantically and her knees went weak. She would have fallen to the floor if it hadn't been for Kalil standing behind her, holding onto her tightly.

"Ssh, Des, it's me. It's Kalil," he whispered in her ear. A single tear slipped down his cheek for the woman he used to love. He'd watched Destiny grow up from a little hot girl chasing ballers on the corner to his baby mother and he still had love for her. He didn't want her to end up like this. "Shh! It's all right. Everything's cool. Just calm down," he stated as she cried in his arms.

He picked her up and took her into the bathroom. He ran her a bath and then washed her as continuous tears graced her face.

"I'm sorry, Kalil. I'm sorry for everything. You tried to tell me about Fatboy—"

"Des, look at what you let that nigga do to you. You were so worried about him that you stopped taking care of our daughter. She was supposed to come first. Even in his grave he got a hold on you. You feel so guilty because of what he did to Jada that you smoking crack. What? You a junkie now?"

"I can't help it."

"Shut that shit up, Destiny. You can help it. You know I can't let Jada be around this, right?"

"Kalil, please don't take her away from me," Destiny begged.

Kalil shook his head from side to side. "I have to, Destiny. I can't let my daughter come up in this environment. In your heart you know that it's the best thing for all of us right now. I've been gone for too long. Let me be a father to my daughter. We'll work on you getting better, and I'll never stop you from seeing Jada, but I can't let her live with you. I have to keep her safe. I never told you this, but I feel guilty too. If I had been in Jada's life, then Fatboy would've never had the opportunity to put his hands on her. He wouldn't have had the opportunity to get his hands on my woman, for that matter. I fucked up when I got sent upstate. Now I've got to make this right."

Kalil lifted her from the bathtub and wrapped a towel around her body. "Now it's time for you to take responsibility for your actions and be a woman, okay?"

For the first time since he was released, Destiny didn't argue back. She nodded her head in agreement. "I love you," she whispered as she held her head down to her chest.

Kalil lifted her head with his finger. "Des, you are the mother of my child. I'll always have love for you, but it's not like that anymore."

Kalil escorted Destiny to the hospital and checked her into a rehabilitation center, and with Destiny's blessing he left with his daughter.

As he headed back to Quinn's his cell phone rang. He checked the caller ID and smiled when he saw June's name flash on the screen. His restless wait was brought to an end. He answered, "What's good, fam?"

"You, baby! I've been trying to get at you, my nigga. I need to discuss something with you. You ready to handle that?"

Kalil knew that June was talking about business and he was more than ready to get his paper right. "Yeah, I'm wit' it. When can we link up?"

"The sooner the better."

"How many you need?" Kalil knew that it really didn't matter. All he had to do was make one phone call and he would be blessed with the bricks.

"We'll talk. Meet me at Central Park by the pink in two hours."

Kalil snapped his cell phone shut and scooped Jada into his arms. "Life gon' be much better for us, I promise," he stated as he headed back toward Quinn's.

"I'm telling you. If you supply the bricks, my man is willing to pay thirty-five a joint." June rubbed his hands together. He and Kalil had met up at the park to discuss business.

Kalil watched as Jada ran anxiously to the play area, where other kids were playing. He reluctantly had to bring her along because he didn't have time to drop her off before the meeting. As he sat in the passenger side of June's cocaine-white Lexus, he listened as his old friend told him about his buyer from D.C.

"Thirty-five a brick?" Kalil knew that he could get the bricks from Hova at twelve apiece, which could turn a $22,000-profit off each one sold. Kalil began to get the old itch that he used to have. He knew the feeling too well, the feeling of coming up on some serious cash.

"Yep. It's a drought going on back home. Niggas can't get their hands on anything good. Cats are paying top dollar for quality dope right now. I know you have a plug on the bricks and this would be a come up, nah mean?" June looked over at Kalil.

Kalil's mind began to race. He glanced at Jada playing on the swings as he thought about what he was about to do. He did the math in his head and realized that he could make a lot of money off just one transaction. "How do you know this cat is serious? Have you dealt with him before?" Kalil asked as he began to play mental chess.

"No doubt. He goes by the name Mateo. I hooked up with him about five years ago, during a bid in Sing Sing. He's a Dominican mu'fucka with long paper. He actually wanted more than thirty, but he wants to see how good the quality is. I told him you had the connect on the best the streets has to offer. When I said you were connected with Hova, he wanted in pronto!" June replied as he was growing more excited by the moment.

"And what do you get out of all of this?" Kalil asked, knowing that June wasn't going to just plug him in without a finder's fee.

"Ten percent, my nigga, of what he spends. So that would be . . . one hundred and five thousand," June said while he smiled at the thought of making some much-needed money.

Kalil respected the rules of the streets and knew that ten percent wasn't a bad due. He weighed the options in his mind, and his conscience had its own session of tug-of-war. *I have to get out of Quinn's house and provide a place for my daughter by hook or crook. Just this one flip and I'm out . . . I'm out,* Kalil thought to himself as he remained silent. "It's a wrap. Contact yo' man and tell him I'll have them on deck," Kalil said as he slowly nodded his head.

"That's what I'm talking about. Let's get this money fam!" June said as he reached out his hand and slapped Kalil's palms. Kalil could see the urgency in June's eyes. It was the same look Kalil used to have when in pursuit of money.

"I'll hit you as soon as I get them," Kalil said as he exited the car. He was about to get paid so he could take care of his daughter and provide for London. He knew that London was meant to be with him and he wasn't going to let a financial problem be the reason why he couldn't be with his soul mate.

"Come on, baby girl, it's time to go," he said as he reached out his hand for his daughter.

Jada put her hands on her tiny hips. "Already, Daddy?"

"Yeah, Daddy got to take care of business, but I promise I'll bring you back soon, okay?"

"Okay."

Jada joined her father as he hailed a cab to make it back to Quinn's house. Kalil was about to drop her off with Roxi and prepare to make his final power move. "Let's get it," Kalil said to himself as he thought about seeing Hova, the man with the "keys to the city."

London sat at the one end of the long dinner table, while Jake sat at the other. The large dining room was silent and she picked at her food as her mind raced.

"Jake, when can I go back to the school?" London knew that if she could get to the school then she would be able to contact Kalil.

"You're not going back to the school. I think that we need to concentrate on our marriage. That school is a distraction to you." Jake calmly picked up his champagne flute and sipped some Dom Pérignon.

"I need to go back, Jake. I love that school. It's the only way I can dance," she pleaded. Out loud she was pleading to dance, but in her heart she was pleading for him to let her out so that she could run to Kalil. She could feel her heart breaking more with each passing day.

"You heard what I said! Why are you so adamant about that damn ghetto-ass school? You're not going back there," Jake stated sternly.

London dropped the subject and decided to approach the situation differently. She could no longer afford to reason with her husband. He'd become too brutal and abusive toward her. Living was no longer what she did. She was surviving, because she knew that it wouldn't be long before Jake lost his temper and killed her. She was going to turn the tables on him. *I have to be the wife that he wants me to be. If I don't, he will never let me out,* she thought to herself.

"I'm sorry, Jake. You're right. I don't need to go back there. All I need is you," London stated with a fake smile.

Jake looked up in surprise as the words slipped from London's tongue. He had gotten so used to her cold and deviant nature toward him.

"I love you."

She stood up and walked toward him. The bruises that covered the right side of her face and neck didn't take away from her exotic beauty.

"I'm sorry, baby. You're my husband and I just want to make you happy." She stood directly in front of him.

Jake removed the linen napkin that lay across his lap and wiped his hands on it before running his hands up and down London's defined hips and thighs. She had the body of a voluptuous stripper, but was toned like a prima ballerina. The feel of her soft skin caused a bulge to form in his Armani slacks.

London winced from his touch. Her entire body was sore, but she knew what she needed to do. "I miss you, Jake. I miss how you make love to me," she whispered as he stood to his feet, running his hands up her body as he arose. He didn't say a word, but London knew that she had him right where she wanted when she saw the lustful look in his eyes.

"Jake, fuck me," she whispered as she took his hand and led him up the stairs. She removed a piece of her clothing with each step that she took until she reached her bedroom. She then began to undress him.

"Hmm," he moaned as he kissed her aggressively while she stroked his penis.

She pushed him down on the bed and straddled him.

"Close your eyes," she said seductively. Her pussy wasn't wet at all. In fact, she was disgusted by the man beneath her, but she had to proceed with her plan.

Jake closed his eyes, and London put her index finger in her mouth, wetting it thoroughly, and then she inserted it into her vagina to make sure that her husband thought she was in the mood. She fingered herself and massaged her clitoris until her juices formed in a puddle on Jake's stomach. She then slid herself down on his pole.

His hands immediately found their place on her hips, and she rode him slowly. Jake matched her motions in his own unique way as he developed a slow rhythm. She turned around, riding him backwards, because she knew that it was his favorite position. She was forced to close her eyes when she felt tears welling up. She couldn't believe that she was doing this.

"Ride it for me, London," he stated as he smacked her firm behind lightly.

I should kill him right now for all the shit he's put me through, she thought as she looked down at Jake, who was enjoying their sexual escapade with his eyes closed. He bit his bottom lip in pleasure. If she had a razor, she probably would have turned her thoughts into actions.

She felt his body tense up and she knew that he was about to explode. London couldn't stand the thought of having his sperm inside of her, so she jumped up and allowed him to release his seed on the bedspread.

"Ohh . . . ohh," he moaned in elation.

She could see him slipping out of consciousness almost instantly, his eyelids half-open.

"I love you," he stated.

She didn't reply, but she lay beside him waiting for him to fall asleep. It never failed. Every time she put it on him, he would be knocked out for hours. She was always able to put him into a deep sleep. It had been so long since she had actually consented to have sex with him, she knew that once she gave him some, he would be out for the count.

"Jake," she called after a half hour of silence. She waited for his response, but when she heard the light snore coming from him, she knew that it was a wrap. It was either now or never. If she didn't make it out of the house that night then she never would. This was her only chance.

She slowly moved from underneath him as the bed squeaked slightly. She frowned as her motion rocked the bed. *God, please let this mu'fucka stay 'sleep,* she prayed silently as she tiptoed around the room. She opened her dresser drawer quietly and pulled out a black and silver BCBG sweatpants and a black baby tee that had the logo across the front in rhinestones. She quickly slipped into the clothing and grabbed a couple more outfits, stuffing them into a gym bag. She grabbed her wedding ring off the dresser, not for sentimental reasons, but because she knew the worth of it. She didn't have one red cent to her name, but she knew that she could get at least ten stacks for her $100,000 ring.

Jake shifted in his sleep as he changed positions, and London almost shit bricks because she thought he would wake up and catch her trying to leave. She stood completely still until she was sure that he was still asleep and then crept with catlike skills down the wraparound staircase, grabbing her keys to her Lexus on her way out the door.

Once she was outside she sprinted to her car, threw her gym bag in the back, and sped up the street as her breathing came out in erratic spurts of energy. Her adrenaline was pumping as her survival instincts kicked into full gear. Although she was nervous as ever as she whipped the luxury car away from Jake, she felt liberated.

Now that she was out of that house there was no way that she was going back. She sped through the streets of New York. She was so anxious to see Kalil that she shed tears as she maneuvered in and out of traffic. She looked at her wedding ring and decided to stop by a local pawnshop first. She knew that she and Kalil would need money in order to get out of town. She was so close to being with the man that she loved, and nothing was going to stand in her way.

Kalil patted his daughter's head softly as she slept soundly in his lap. He knew what he was about to do was risky. If he got caught, he would be facing a life sentence in a federal penitentiary. He tried to not think of the what-ifs and focus on what was. The fact was he was broke. He was struggling to maintain and stay out of the game when everybody knew that he was born to move keys. It was what he did best. Getting money the illegal way was Kalil's specialty, and now that he had taken Jada from her mother, he definitely needed to come up on some serious cash.

June's hookup seemed to be the best way to do it. It was a one-time flip. *All I got to do is make it happen . . . make this money.* Kalil dialed the first three numbers to Hova's cell. He hesitated as he stared down at his daughter. *Be a man. You ain't ever been scared of this money before. Look at Jada, she's counting on you. You can't even get your woman because your pockets ain't healthy,* he told himself as he thought of Jada and London at the same time.

Quinn entered the apartment and noticed that Kalil was sitting in the dark. "You a'ight, fam?"

"Yeah, I'm good. Just thinking about this run. I love this little girl right here, man." Kalil became emotional, and a tear slid from his eyes. He sniffed loudly and wiped the tear away quickly. "I can't go back upstate."

"Yo, I'm not trying to see you get sent back up. You sure you want to fuck with that nigga June? I know he's your peoples and all, but I don't trust him."

"I know, fam. I know you feel some kind of way about my man, June, but I think June is one hunnid. I'm not really trying to get my hands dirty like this again, but I'm a man. I got to take care of my daughter. I've been down long enough. You don't know how that shit feels, yo, to be a grown man crawling in society. I got to stand on my own two again, nah mean?"

"I would still feel much better if you let me roll. I know that I got your back, no matter what pop off. I can't say the same for your man, June."

"Nah, bro. I need you here. If some shit do pop off, I gotta know that there's someone still here to take care of my shorty. She's my world. I'm gon' always be here, through her. As long as she's straight, that's all that matters."

It was at that moment that he decided to go through with June's plan. He flipped up the face to his cell and dialed Hova's number.

"Hello?"

"Yo, Hov, this Kalil."

"Kalil, how have things been for you? That legit role must not be working out too well if you're calling me," Hova stated playfully.

"Nah, I'm ready to do me again, that's all. I know I haven't been in the loop for a while, but is that discount still good?"

"The party is still at twelve o'clock," Hova responded in code, letting Kalil know that the price for the bricks was twelve thousand apiece. "How many guests?"

"Thirty," Kalil replied. "They on deck?"

"Yeah. I can drop 'em off to you in about an hour."

Kalil gave Hova directions to Quinn's apartment building and then hung up the phone. The feeling that was racing through his body was a mixture of anxiety and regret, but the deal was already done—Hova was on his way.

Kalil lifted Jada's head off his lap and stood up. He knelt beside her, kissed her forehead, and watched her sleep peacefully. He prayed to God that he'd come back home to her.

***

"I'll give you three thousand for it," the old white woman with bifocal glasses stated.

London frowned in exasperation as she put her hand on her hip and replied, "Three thousand? Come on, you know that's not a fair price. That ring is worth at least a hundred thousand. The least I can give it to you for is twenty grand."

The old woman looked at the bruised face of the girl that stood before her. She knew that however much she agreed to give the young girl, it would be all that she had to depend on. Working in her profession, the old woman had seen plenty of young girls who were willing to pawn their most prized possessions just to get some quick escape money. She looked with pity at the desperate girl and replied, "I'll give you fifteen."

"Deal," London replied as she placed the ring on the glass countertop. She didn't think twice about trading it in. Most women would have had some type of attachment to their wedding ring. London saw hers as a shackle and she'd just been freed from its confinement. Now all she had to do was get to Kalil. She wished that she had his number so that she could let him know that she was coming, but she said, "Fuck it," and decided that she would explain everything when she saw him face-to-face.

She almost thought about trading in her car so that she and Kalil would have more money, but figured that she should just get Kalil first. *He can take care of everything else. He will know what to do,* she thought as she nervously drove toward his place. London was terrified and her heart beat erratically. She kept checking her rearview mirror to see if Jake had sent anyone after her yet. She had only been gon' for an hour, but she figured that it wouldn't take her husband long to figure out that she was missing. She hoped that by the time he woke up, she would be heading down I-95, driving as far away as the four wheels of her Lexus coupe would take her.

Kalil leaned against the brick building, one leg bent, his foot resting against the wall as he patiently waited for Hova to arrive. He watched as the black '08 Cadillac DeVille pulled up and parked near the curb. He knew that it was Hova. The luxury vehicle stood out like a sore thumb in the run-down neighborhood. He looked both ways up the block to make sure that prying eyes weren't watching before he stepped toward the car.

Hova's driver exited the vehicle and opened the door for Kalil.

"What's up, Hov?" Kalil sat down on the plush leather seats.

"I'm glad that you decided to get back with me. I take it you're ready to get this money again?" Hova asked, a sly smile on his face. He knew that Kalil was capable of moving more keys than any of his other clients. He knew that if Kalil stepped back into the game then he would benefit from it.

"You know how I get down. An opportunity arose to make some easy money. You know I wasn't gon' turn it down." Kalil wasn't trying to engage in small talk, so he cut straight to the point. "You got that?"

"Yeah, my young boy, Peanut, followed me here. The bricks are in his trunk. How long you think it'll be before I get my money?" Hova didn't have a problem giving Kalil the bricks on consignment because he was confident that Kalil was good for it.

"'Bout a week," Kalil replied. The deal was going down that night, but Kalil wanted to give himself a little breathing room with Hova, just in case something popped off.

Hova nodded his head, pulled out a cigar, and hit the unlock button as he watched Kalil get out the car.

"I'ma get at you," Kalil stated before he jogged over to Peanut's car, which was parked a couple feet away.

Peanut leaned out of the window and slapped hands with Kalil. "What's the deal, Kalil? You making moves without da kid?" he asked half jokingly.

"Nah, son, it ain't like that. If I was making moves, you know I'd take you with me. I just got some business to handle with my man, that's all." Kalil walked toward the back of the car and hit the hood lightly, signaling Peanut to pop the trunk.

Peanut hit the button in his dash and Kalil opened the trunk to find three large black duffel bags sitting inside. He peeped his surroundings one more time before he lifted the bags from the trunk and walked across the street. "I'ma get at you, Nut!" he shouted as he jogged across the street and walked into his building to prepare for the drive to D.C. that night.

Hova watched as Kalil took the duffel bags from Peanut's car. He made sure that everything was one hundred with Kalil, keeping his eye on the drop until Kalil was safe inside the building.

"Everything all good, Jake?" one of his loyal disciples asked as he turned the ignition forward on the car, preparing to leave.

"What did I tell you about that *Jake* shit?" Hova stated sternly. He had established his hood name, Hova, a long time ago and hated when people referred to him by his government name.

"My bad, Hov," his disciple replied.

"Let's go," Hova instructed in an annoyed tone of voice. He sat back and rested his eyes as they pulled away from the curb.

"Yo, Hov, ain't that your wife?" the disciple who sat beside Hova in the backseat asked as he eyed the woman who was passing them by.

Hova sat straight up in his seat and peered out of the tinted windows. His temper flared when he saw her. *What is she doing out of the house? She thinks I am just going to sit idly while she runs out on me. I've already told her there is no escaping me,* he thought to himself. *Bitch must think I'm a joke or something. What the fuck is she doing on this side of town anyway?* "Make a right at this corner and swing back around," Hova instructed calmly, not wanting to reveal his anger to his disciple.

"Time's up!"

The sound of the guard's voice snapped Ashley and JaQuavis out of their trance. They'd been listening to Kalil's story for the past two hours and were completely awed by it. Visitors were only supposed to have thirty minutes of visiting time, but JaQuavis slipped the floor guard a Benjamin Franklin to let them overstay their time.

"Damn, that's so fucked-up," Ashley said as she held her hand over her mouth. "So Jake was Hova? You were fucking with his woman and didn't even know it!"

"Yeah, I didn't have a clue." Kalil crossed his hands and looked back and forth at the two authors.

JaQuavis wanted to hear more. "So what happened after that? Did he try to get at you after he found out?"

"Time's up!"

The guard walked over to Kalil and forcefully picked him up by his arm. "I said it's time to go!"

"We will be here next visiting day," JaQuavis assured as he watched the guard carry Kalil away. His story was so intriguing and interesting that they were itching to hear more, but now all they could do was wait.

Next Visiting Day

Ashley and JaQuavis walked to the table that Kalil was sitting at, but this time they came prepared with notepads and pens. Kalil wanted to share his story with the world and they were going to help him do just that. Kalil didn't waste any time. Without even saying hello, he picked up right where he left off.

***

As London approached the high-rise project building, her heart began to beat uncontrollably. She parked her car on the side of the street, hitting her alarm as she got out and rushed into the building. *Please let him be here,* she thought as she took the elevator up to the sixth floor.

She stood in front of Kalil's door and thought about what she was about to do. By leaving her husband she'd just put her life in danger and she prayed that she could get out of New York before he could find her. She took a deep breath and lifted her hands to knock on the door.

Kalil heard the knock on the door and immediately rose to answer it. He didn't want the sound to awake his daughter from her slumber.

Quinn poked his head out of the bedroom door. "You got that?"

"Yeah, I got it," Kalil replied as Quinn closed his door and returned to his room.

Kalil opened the door and the sight of London standing before him broke his heart in half. She had so many bruises on her face and neck, the sight alone made murderous thoughts run through his mind.

She stood in his doorstep with her head down.

"He hurt me, Kalil. I can't take this anymore. I can't go back there. He's going to kill me one day." Her voice cracked as all of her fear, frustrations, and anger surfaced, and a fountain of tears appeared in her eyes.

Kalil grabbed her hand and pulled her close. "I'm sorry. I shouldn't have let you go back there," he whispered in her ear as he held her body gently.

Her head rested on his shoulder as she continued to talk. "He tried to throw me out of the car, Kalil. We were driving down the expressway and he told me to get out! He's going to kill me. I know he is."

"Ssh, he's not going to kill you, ma. I'm not gon' let nothing happen to you. Why didn't you call me?" Kalil stepped back slightly so he could look her in the eyes. He cupped her face in his hands and kissed her on the lips. "I would have come for you."

"I couldn't. I think he found your number. I know he did, because I couldn't find it anywhere, and he's been flipping out on me."

"Fuck this, yo. Where he rest at? It's time for me to see this nigga." Kalil walked over to the coat closet and pulled his .45 from up top.

"Kalil, no! Please, I just want to leave here," London begged.

Kalil could see that her fear had taken control of her, and he held onto her tightly as he tried to calm her down. "Okay, okay. How do you want me to handle this?"

London looked up at him, her vision blurry from crying. "Kalil, I'm in love with you. I love you, and after spending time with you, I can't stay in my situation. I don't know if you feel the same way that I do, but you showed me how a relationship is supposed to be, Kalil. I need you in my life. I've never been happy before I met you. I don't care where we go. I just want to leave New York."

Kalil took a deep breath and released it slowly. He was tired of watching London get hurt at the hands of her husband, but he knew that it was better for him if he just took her away from the situation.

"I love you," she whispered.

Kalil pulled London into the kitchen. "Listen, ma—" He picked her up as if she were a child and sat her down on top of the counter, then eased himself between her legs. "I've been feeling you since the first time I saw you. I've watched this nigga hurt you repeatedly, and every time I've had to swallow my pride because you asked me to step off. I love you, ma."

London's eyes looked hopeful when she heard the words *I love you* leave his mouth, and Kalil peeped the way that she looked up at him in surprise.

"Yeah, London, I love you. I want to take you away from everybody that has hurt you."

"I have some money. We can leave."

Kalil wanted nothing more than to leave this city with London and his daughter by his side, but he couldn't go from one hood to the next hood. He wanted to be able to provide a better life for London.

London saw the look of doubt that crossed his face. "Please, Kalil, I can't do this without you. I need you in my life."

Kalil nodded his head. "Okay."

"Okay?" London asked in surprise.

"We can leave town, but you got to let me get my money up. I've got something set up with my man from D.C. I got to deliver these bricks." He saw the skeptical look that crossed her face. "I promise you, one run and I'm out the game for good," he whispered as he caressed her cheek. "I love you. I need you behind me. I swear, we'll blow town tomorrow night, a'ight?"

"Okay." London grabbed his hand and kissed it gently, holding onto him as if she would never see him again. "Promise me that everything will be all right. Promise that you will come back to me."

"I promise, London." Kalil grabbed one of her hands and placed it on the left side of his chest.

He then pressed his hand against her heart and finished: *"We gon'* be all right. No man will ever put his hands on you again. I'ma take care of you, and you never have to worry about me putting my hands on you. I'm a man and I'm gon' treat you like my queen. You the only woman that has been able to get inside here." Kalil thumped his chest, referring to his heart.

"You're the only man that I've ever loved," London whispered as she stared intensely at the one man she'd given her heart to.

"Then that's all that matters. As long as I'm in your heart and you are in mine, our love won't die. I need you to trust me on this. Let me go make this money, and tomorrow we're ghost."

London nodded her head and kissed Kalil passionately. She knew at that exact moment that Kalil was truly the man that she'd been praying to meet. She didn't care that she hadn't known him that long. She knew that their love was real, and even if she died tomorrow, just the fact that she was loved by him today was enough for her to die a happy woman.

Kalil sat on the couch in silence, his daughter's head resting in his lap and London's head resting on his shoulder. He gripped her hand as he thought about what he was willing to risk for the pursuit of money. He knew that he needed to make it happen for his family.

His phone rang loudly, interrupting their intimate moment. He stared at London as he answered, "Hello?"

"It's me, homeboy. I'm outside," June stated.

Kalil flipped his phone down and headed for the door. There was no turning back now.

Hova sat in the back of his Cadillac and waited patiently as he smoked his Cuban cigar, his car parked inconspicuously up the block as he waited for London to emerge from the apartment building. *This bitch wants to hide in this mu'fucka. She thinks she gon' get away from me. I own her.*

Hova immediately sat up in his seat when he saw a white Lexus pull up in front of the apartment building. He then noticed Kalil come out of the building toting the duffel bags full of cocaine. He figured that Kalil was going to handle his business and was prepared to let him do his thing until he saw London come out of the building behind him.

"Be careful," London stated as she hugged Kalil tightly. "Make sure you come back to me, Kalil. I love you more than anything in this world."

A tear fell from her eyes, and he wiped it away. "I love you too," Kalil replied. "Go upstairs and lock the doors. Quinn is cool with it. Just take care of Jada and get some rest. I'll be back before you know it." He hugged her tightly, kissed her forehead, and smacked her ass lightly.

Kalil watched her walk back into the apartment building. He had no idea that he was crossing the very man that had put him on. London, the woman that Kalil loved, was Hova's wife and he didn't even know it.

"Dammmn! He baggin' your bitch?" the backseat disciple asked in disbelief as he stared out of the tinted window.

The words were too much for Hova to bear, and before he could stop himself he had fired two hollow-tip bullets through the side of his disciple's head.

The disciple in the front seat turned around and almost vomited from the gruesome scene. Brain matter was splattered all over the back-passenger window. Afraid that he'd be next, he remained silent as Hova's heavy, erratic breathing filled the car.

Hova's chrome 9 mm with the silencer smoked as he stared at the corpse before him. "Don't you ever disrespect me! Ever!" he shouted in rage as he fired two more shots into the already dead young man.

Murderous intentions became Hova's focus as he watched London and Kalil. The disrespect that he felt when he saw the way his wife looked at Kalil was enough to drive him insane. He didn't give a damn why she chose to cheat. London was his property, and Kalil had trespassed.

"Handle that," Hova said to his disciple sitting in the front seat.

"How you want me to approach it?"

Hova reached in the front seat and smacked his disciple upside his head. "Murder the mu'fucka! Fuck you mean, how I want you to approach it?" he yelled out in anger.

"I'm just saying . . . that's your wife, B."

He responded without hesitation. "Get rid of that bitch too. Get me out of here," he said, and he leaned low in his seat as the car pulled away.

Chapter Eleven

June pushed his whip down I-95 as the bass from his speakers caused the whole car to vibrate.

Kalil was uneasy, knowing that he was on probation and riding around with thirty bricks of cocaine in the trunk. He looked over at June and noticed that he looked edgy. June kept on checking the mirrors and was real jittery and he was sweating profusely, even though the AC was blasting on high.

"You good, fam?" Kalil checked the rearview mirror for cops.

June checked the rearview mirror again. "Y-yeah, I'm good. What you keep on checking the mirrors for, son?" he asked nervously.

"Nigga, because we riding dirty. Fuck you mean?" Kalil shook his head and focused on the road ahead. He was getting an ill feeling from June. June seemed to be nervous, like it was his first time flipping birds. *This nigga is an amateur. Look at him, over there sweating bullets.*

Just as Kalil finished his thought, June reached into his glove compartment and pulled out a small baggy full of cocaine. He emptied a small pile between his index finger and thumb as he tried to steer the vehicle.

Kalil watched as June took a hit of the blow. "Fall back, nigga! What you doing?"

"I'm trying to calm myself, man. Damn! Chill out. Let me do me." June glared at Kalil.

Kalil didn't want to get into the drama, so he just remained silent and thought about the money he was about to make. If it was any other time, Kalil would've got at his ass for getting "flip-lip." But at that moment Kalil was in his hustler mode and wasn't trying to rock the boat.

"Just be easy on that shit. I don't rock with that shit. I like to stay focused while handling business, nah mean?" Kalil thought about Jada and London, the only two people he needed for his own happiness.

June took a sudden right turn, getting off at a rest area. He recklessly steered the vehicle to the detour.

Kalil sat up and frowned. "Fuck you doing?"

"I got to piss, son. I have been holding my shit for the last hour." June pulled into the vacant parking lot.

"Hurry up, fam. We shouldn't be making any unnecessary stops," Kalil stated in an aggravated tone as he watched June exit the car and jog to the restroom. Kalil was getting tired of June's erratic behavior and instantly regretted doing business with the fool. *I knew I shouldn't have fucked with this cat. He ain't good business.* Kalil closed his eyes and threw his head back in the seat.

Whack! The butt of June's pistol went across Kalil's temple.

Kalil saw stars, and his vision was slightly blurred. He hadn't noticed that June had crept around to the passenger side and snuck up on him.

June pointed the pistol at Kalil. "Get the fuck out of the car!" he yelled as he wiped his running nose.

Kalil was completely taken off guard. "What the fuck are you doing?" he asked as he tried to regain his blurred vision.

June opened Kalil's door and pulled him out of the car.

Kalil fell to his knees and finally staggered to his feet. "June! What's yo' problem, son?" He put both of his hands in front of him. Kalil couldn't believe what was happening. His head ached from the unanticipated blow from the gun and blood trickled from his forehead.

"Shut the fuck up! Get on your knees." June waved his pistol wildly at Kalil and wiped his nose again.

"Yo, man, this ain't the way to be, fam. Just take the bricks, man."

"I'm playin' fo' keeps, fam. I gotta get mine! You always used to brag about how you was the man. Now I'm about to be the man, son. Say good night!" June cocked back the hammer on the gun.

"Wait! June—"

Boom, boom, boom, boom! June let off four bullets directly into Kalil's chest, jerking his body left to right. The hollow-tip bullets left Kalil lying motionless in the middle of the parking lot.

Thoughts of Jada ran through Kalil's mind as the bullets hit him one by one, leaving him facing the sky with his eyes closed.

June then jumped in his car, leaving Kalil slumped in the lot. He was on his way back home with a truckful of opportunity.

Quinn watched as June's car whipped out of the lot. He had been tailing them for the whole trip, but June had shook him off a couple miles back. His suspicions about June wouldn't let him leave his cousin without backup. Quinn looked more closely and realized that June was in the car by himself, and he immediately grew nervous.

He sped his car into the lot and saw his cousin lying motionless in the middle of the parking lot. "Kalil!" Quinn yelled at the top of his lungs. His eyes began to water and his hands shook uncontrollably. He sped over to Kalil, jumped out of the car, and ran to his side. He stood over his cousin's body and his legs got weak.

Just as he was about to drop to his knees, Kalil twitched.

"Kalil! Where you hit?" Quinn asked, since no blood was visible.

Kalil wheezed for air as he opened his eyes and stared at his best friend and cousin.

Quinn dropped to his knees and began to feel on Kalil to see where the wound was located, but to no avail. He couldn't find it. He grabbed Kalil's chest and felt a bulletproof vest. He ripped open Kalil's shirt and exposed the vest with four bullets lodged in it.

"I'm good, I'm good. It just knocked the breath out of me." Kalil slowly sat up, wincing in pain, immediately grateful for his cousin's suspicions.

In Kalil's day, he always put on a vest for protection, and his intuition told him to strap one on for this trip. His decision was lifesaving. "He got away?" Kalil asked in a raspy voice, still trying to catch his breath.

"Yeah, he got away. Not for long, though."
Quinn helped Kalil into his car. He wanted to
go after June, but he knew it would be pointless
since June was long gone by now.

"Fuck!" Kalil yelled as he came to the realization that June had gotten off with thirty kilos of
cocaine. To make matters worse, he still owed
Hova money for the consignment.

Quinn looked over at Kalil, who dropped his
head into his palms. "What? What?"

Kalil whispered, "Hova," as he shook his head
from side to side.

Quinn already knew what Kalil meant as the
name came out of his mouth. To owe Hova was
to start making funeral arrangements for yourself. Kalil's world had changed course in a matter
of minutes. What looked to be the beginning of
a dream started to seem more like the start of a
nightmare.

"Fuck, man!" Kalil cursed himself for ever
trusting June. He was so close to getting out of
the game for good, but this one event had put
him in the hole for more than a quarter million.

Quinn was speechless. He didn't know exactly
what to say. *I told his ass about that D.C. nigga.
I told him.* Quinn looked down at Kalil. He could
tell by the look on Kalil's face that he was messed
up in the head right now.

Quickly doing the math in his head, he figured that Kalil owed Hova $360,000 and he knew that Hova would want every single penny. He knew it wasn't the time for "I told you so."

"So what you want to do? Whatever we got to do, let's make it happen, son. You know I'm with you, no matter what. If we need to get at this nigga June we can get to it. If we got to settle this with Hova we can get at him too. Just say the word," Quinn stated, even though he knew that going against Hova was a guaranteed death sentence.

"I don't even know, Quinn," Kalil said as he removed the bulletproof vest. "I don't know. I just need some time to get my head together."

"You need to fall back for a day or two. We can't go back to the apartment. Once Hov don't hear from you, he gon' know what's up, and that's the first place he gon' look. As a matter of fact, we need to get Jada and ol' girl out of there too."

Kalil knew that Quinn was right. He had to keep his daughter and London safe. He pulled out his cell and dialed Quinn's house.

London picked up on the first ring. "Hello?" she answered.

"London, it's me, Kalil."

"Is everything all right?"

Kalil paused and closed his eyes at the sound of her voice. He loved the woman on the other end of the phone. She was his other half and he had to take care of her.

"Kalil? You're scaring me. Are you okay?" she asked after a lengthy silence.

"I'm good, ma. Everything's good. I need you to do me a favor."

"Anything."

"Take Jada and go to the hotel that I took you to on Lexington Avenue. Stay there until you hear from me. This business is going to take a couple days," he said in an assertive tone. He didn't want her to be worried about him, so he didn't tell her the full story.

"Are you sure you're okay?" she asked, her voice full of concern.

"I'm okay, I promise, but do what I told you and take care of Jada for me." Kalil hung up the phone before she could respond. He had to get her out of his mind. He couldn't focus on London and Hova at the same time. She was a beautiful distraction to have, but at the moment he needed to be about his paper.

London rushed to the couch, where Jada rested, and shook her gently. "Jada," she whispered in the child's ear. She gazed lovingly at Kalil's daughter and secretly wished that she was her mother. She knew that Kalil loved his little girl tremendously and she vowed that if anything ever happened to him, she would take care of Jada as if she were her own.

"Jada, it's time to get up, sweetheart," she said.

Jada squirmed and rubbed her eyes. "Ms. London," she asked as she blinked repeatedly to get the sleep out of her eyes, "where's my daddy?"

"He had to go out for a while. He'll be back in a day or so, but until then it's just us girls." Even though London was worried about Kalil, she didn't want to make Jada think that anything was wrong. "I have an idea. You want to go to a hotel and have a sleepover?"

"Ohh yeah!" Jada exclaimed in excitement. She sat up instantly. "Is there a pool? Can I swim too?"

"You sure can. Come on, let's get up and get dressed, so we can hurry up and leave." London smiled.

London helped Jada dress. She couldn't stop her hands from shaking, she was so nervous. She knew that as soon as she escaped New York, everything would be better. She would be able to calm down and move on to a better life with Kalil. She just had to make it to that point.

She helped Jada slip on her clothes and grabbed their bags. "Come on, sweetie." London held out her hand for Jada, and they headed out to the hotel.

***

"Yo, son, there she is!" Lynch tapped Peanut, who had nodded off in the passenger seat of the tinted Monte Carlo.

Hova had plans for his cheating wife. Her disloyalty was unacceptable and because of it he knew that he had to get rid of her. She knew too much about him and his business and could no longer be trusted. So he put two of his most loyal disciples on London. Hova was sure that there would be no hesitation when it came to them handling her. There was no way that he could let her live. On top of that, his ego was bruised and he had to give her what she had coming to her—death.

Peanut sat up in his chair and noticed London as she walked out of the apartment building with bags in one hand. She seemed to be in a rush and was practically dragging a little girl along with her. He watched as she loaded the bags into her car and safely buckled the little girl inside.

"Yeah, she about to get hers." Lynch pulled out an automatic AR-15 that was sure to put London to sleep.

Peanut peered closer and noticed the little girl's face. *Oh shit, that's little Jada,* he thought to himself. He didn't know why Kalil's daughter was with Hova's wife, but he knew that he couldn't allow Lynch to pull the trigger. "Hova ain't say nothing about no little girl."

"Ain't nothing personal. Lil' mama just in the wrong place at the wrong time," Lynch replied as he loaded the weapon.

"Yo, hold up on that shit. You know how Hov is. We got to follow his instructions to the T," Peanut argued, trying to stall for time. He couldn't just sit back and watch Lynch murder Kalil's daughter.

If it wasn't for Kalil bringing him up in the game, Peanut knew that he wouldn't be the man he was today. *What the fuck is she doing with Hova's wife?* he thought to himself. "He ain't say anything about killing no kids. I mean, you can go ahead and do what you feel, but you know if you do it incorrectly, it's gon' be your ass on the chopping block," Peanut said, playing mental chess with the seasoned killer in front of him. He knew that if he made it seem like Hova would be upset then Lynch might back down.

Lynch stuck his head out the window and eyed London. "Damn, it ain't nothing worse than having an itch you can't scratch. Right now my trigger finger is itching, nah mean? Call Hova and see what he want us to do."

Peanut pulled out his cell phone and dialed his own voice mail. There was no way he was going to call Hova because he already knew what the answer would be. "Yo, Hov, this Nut. Hit me back ASAP. There's a wrench in the plan," he said. Peanut hung up the phone and looked at Lynch. "Nigga didn't answer the phone. I don't know 'bout you, but I'm not trying to make a wrong move, nah mean? I say we wait until he calls us back before we do anything."

"I feel that." Lynch put his gun underneath his seat. "We better tail this bitch, though. It looks like she trying to hide out, and we need to know where to find her when Hova do call."

Peanut wanted to lose London to ensure Jada's safety, but he figured that Lynch would grow suspicious if he changed the plan too much. *At least they ain't circled in chalk,* he thought. He nodded his head. "A'ight, let's roll. Make sure you ain't following her too close."

London drove with one hand on the bottom of her steering wheel, and Jada clung to the other one as they rode down the city streets. She rubbed the back of Jada's hand as she looked over at the little girl sitting beside her. She couldn't wait to begin her new life with Jada and Kalil. It was what she always wanted—a man who loved her to the depths of her being and a child to care for. *Maybe one day Kalil and I can give Jada a little brother or sister.*

She parked on Fiftieth Street and walked around the car to let Jada out. She grabbed their bags out of the backseat and then made her way into the hotel.

***

Lynch tried to lean his seat back to make himself more comfortable in the car. They had been sitting on Lexington Avenue for two hours, and he was growing more impatient with every passing minute. "Why he ain't called yet?"

"Just chill out, fam. He gon' call." Peanut pulled out a spliff and prepared to gut the inside. He knew that he was playing with Lynch, making him wait for a phone call that would never come. With expertise he rolled a Dutch and sparked it up. He could tell that Lynch was irritated by his demeanor. He hit the blunt, held the smoke in his lungs, and then held it up for Lynch to partake. "Calm yo' ass down and hit this shit," Peanut told him.

Lynch shook his head. "Don't nobody fuck with weed no more, nigga. That mild shit doesn't even get me high, fam." He pulled out a small plastic coke-filled baggie. "This right here gon' get your boy right."

Peanut frowned. He didn't know that Lynch got down like that. *This basehead mu'fucka . . .* Peanut shook his head. "I don't mess around with that. Today you hitting coke, next week your ass will be smoking rocks."

Lynch laughed it off as if it was a joke, but Peanut was dead serious. He had learned that golden rule from Kalil. A coke habit was something that he never wanted to have.

"This here will give your scary ass some balls," Lynch added.

"A'ight, mu'fucka. You feeling good," Peanut replied, giving Lynch a pass on the slick shit he'd just said.

Before Lynch could respond, his cell phone rang. He checked the caller ID and a smirk crossed his face. "It's Hov."

Peanut quickly grabbed the phone from Lynch's hand. He didn't want his white lie to be discovered. "Let me talk to this mu'fucka," he stated as he flipped up the face. "Hov!" he answered as Lynch looked on in anticipation.

Hova asked, "Did you take care of my little problem for me?"

"Nah, we ran into a little situation. She got a kid with her," Peanut said, hoping that Hova would wait for a better time to get at London.

"I don't care who's with her. Grab her and the kid and take them to one of the money spots. Keep them there until you hear from me."

Peanut hung up the phone and shook his head. He knew that he could no longer stall. Hova had given the order. Now he and Lynch had to follow through.

"What he say?"

"Snatch the bitch and the kid. We've got to take them to one of the stash spots."

"That's what the fuck I'm talking about. You ready to rock, son?"

"Let's roll, baby," Peanut replied hesitantly as he gave his man a pound.

Jada sat Indian-style on the bed and watched attentively as London stood in front of the mirror and pulled her hair up into a neat bun. "Ms. London, did you steal my daddy from my mommy?"

London looked at Jada's reflection and turned toward her. "Jada, what would make you ask that?"

Before that moment London hadn't thought twice about how her relationship with Kalil was affecting Jada.

"I don't know," she replied with a shrug. "Before my daddy went to jail he loved Mommy. Ever since he met you, he don't like her anymore. What if you make him don't like me too?"

London smiled at Jada and made her way over to her. She sat down on the bed beside her. "Jada, I love your father very much, and I know that he cares a lot about me too. I haven't known your father for very long, but I do know that he loves you more than anyone in this entire world."

Jada began to beam with pride as she listened to London speak.

London laughed and put her arms around Jada. "You are his pride and joy, sweetheart, and I would never do anything to try and take your father away from you. And you know what?"

"What?"

"I love you too. I would like to be a part of your family, if you'd let me. Can I share your father's heart with you?" London asked. It was important for her to have Jada's blessing because she knew how important Kalil's daughter was to him. She never wanted Jada to feel threatened or feel that she had to compete to keep her father's love.

"Yeah, I guess I can share him."

"Well, thank you very much." London hugged the little girl. "Now I'm going to go and take a shower so that we can get ready for bed."

"What about swimming?" Jada asked.

"It's too late to go tonight, but I promise that will be the first thing we do tomorrow."

Jada nodded happily and began to bounce on the bed. "I'm going swimming, I'm going swimming," she sang, making London chuckle at her antics.

London was about to go into the bathroom when Jada said, "Ms. London, I'm hungry."

London pulled out the phone book and quickly located a pizza restaurant. "You like pizza?" she asked.

Jada nodded and London placed the delivery order.

"Okay, Jada, I'm about to take a shower. When the deliveryman gets here, come and get me so I can pay for it."

"Okay," Jada said as she watched London enter the bathroom and close the door behind her.

"Aye, my man, I'm looking for my wife. We're vacationing here, and I just flew in on a separate flight. I can't remember what room number she told me she was in and I can't reach her on her cell phone," Lynch lied as he looked innocently into the concierge's eyes.

Peanut stood on the outside of the hotel and peered in as he watched Lynch interact with the man behind the check-in desk. He flipped the face of his cell and attempted to reach Kalil.

The automated voice told him for the umpteenth time, *"The Nextel subscriber that you are trying to reach is unavailable. Please try your call again later."*

Peanut quickly redialed the number one more time, more out of desperation than anything. *Where the fuck is this nigga?* This time he got the voice mail.

"Yo, you've reached Kalil. Leave a message."

"Yo, Kalil, this Peanut. I need you to hit me back ASAP, fam. This is important. It's about your shorty." Peanut hung up the phone and turned back toward the hotel. "Oh shit!" he exclaimed as he bumped directly into Lynch, who was standing closely behind him. "Fuck, nigga! What the fuck you doing, yo, sneaking up on me and shit?"

Peanut was hoping that Lynch hadn't heard the message he'd just left for Kalil.

"You good?" Lynch asked.

"Yeah, I'm good." Peanut peered at Lynch. "Is you good? Did you find out the room number?"

"Yeah, I got it."

"Fuck we standing out here for then?" Peanut asked sarcastically as he walked into the hotel. *Kalil, you runnin' out of time, baby. Where you at?* Peanut didn't want to bring harm to Kalil's little girl, but he knew that if he went against the grain, it would establish beef between himself and Hova, something he didn't want. If it came down to it, he would have to handle his business. He knew that he didn't have a choice. It was all in the game.

***

Tap, tap, tap!

Jada jumped up as soon as she heard the knocking at the door. She was so hungry, she could eat an entire cow. "It's about time," she whined. "Ms. London, food's here!" she called out. She walked over to the door and opened it without hesitation. Her smile was quickly covered by a firm hand, and she was forced back into the room.

"Hmm, hmm!" Her cries were muffled by the two men who rushed into the room with their guns drawn.

"Shut the fuck up!" Lynch whispered harshly. He pulled out the chair from underneath the corner desk, sat the little girl down in it, and pressed the gun to her head.

Peanut's conscience ate at him as he saw the little girl's eyes swell with tears.

"Shut the fuck up, brat, before I blow your brains all over the room."

Lynch's words only made Jada cry harder. She began to sob heavily as she tried to stop herself from crying.

Lynch heard the shower running and knew that Hova's wife was in the bathroom. He sat down on the bed with his gun aimed at Jada as he patiently waited for London to emerge.

London turned off the running water. She stepped out of the shower and began to lotion her body down, applying her favorite Victoria's Secret scent. She paused when she didn't hear the sound of the television going in the room. "Jada, everything okay in there?" She quickly stepped into her satin pink-and-green polka-dot pajama pants and white camisole top. "Jada!" she called again.

London gathered her personal items off of the vanity and exited the bathroom. As soon as she opened the door she was greeted by the barrel of a pistol. Before she even had the chance to scream, she was backhanded to the floor. She looked up and immediately recognized the face of one of her husband's disciples. *He found me,* she thought. She glanced over at a frightened Jada, who was forced to sit still in the chair and was also being held at gunpoint. London knew very well the type of people her husband had working for him. Lynch she knew personally. She'd heard stories of his murder sprees. She silently wished that her husband had sent any other disciple besides him.

London did the only thing that she could think of: pull her wifey card. "What are you doing? I want to speak to my husband now!" She tried to sound as if she wasn't frightened, even though she was silently counting the minutes left in her young life.

"Oh, now you want to speak to Hova? Now this bitch wants to talk to Hova." Lynch pointed at London and looked back at Peanut. "Guess what? Hova sent us."

Lynch wasn't telling London anything that she didn't already know. She had run away and had hoped to leave town before he could catch up with her. Now it was too late.

"Let me just speak to him, please," she cried. "Just let me call him."

Peanut cut in. "Maybe we should let her call."

"What?"

Peanut shrugged. "It ain't gon' hurt nothing. Let the bitch have what she wants. Hova still gon' murder her." He was hoping that once Hova heard his wife's voice he would call off the hit. It was a long shot, but he figured it was worth a try.

"Whatever . . . but she talking on speaker." Lynch flipped out his phone and dialed Hova's number. He knelt down and grabbed London by the hair as he put the phone up to her lips.

Hova answered, "I hope you're calling me to tell me that my problem is taken care of," making it obvious that he'd checked the caller ID.

"Jake?" London stated with fear in her voice. "Jake, baby, what are you doing? I wasn't leaving. I just needed some time to clear my head. Please stop this," she begged.

"London, London, London, you disobeyed me."

"I didn't, Jake. I was going to come back. I just needed time to get my head together. You know that I love you. I would never leave you," she lied. "I took a vow to love you forever. You know our marriage means everything to me."

He could hear the desperation in her voice, and a smile spread across his face. He was amused with her Oscar-worthy attempt to get him to change his mind. "Vows? I must have missed the part where you vowed to be a lying bitch. Or the part where you vowed to have an affair."

Tears flooded London's eyes as she slowly came to the realization of what this was really about. *Oh my God, he knows about Kalil,* she thought to herself.

Hova asked, "Did you enjoy fucking Kalil?"

"Jake, please . . . don't do this," she whispered. She knew that her husband was a cold man and that there was no way he was going to let her live after her betrayal.

After a long silence on the line, Jake finally said to his disciples, "Finish the job. Till death do us part," he stated mockingly before hanging up the phone.

"You heard what he said. Get the fuck up." Lynch pulled London to her feet. He licked his lips as he looked her up and down. Her nipples were hard from the cold chill that had taken over her body. "I'm gon' bless you with this dick before you die," he whispered as he openly lusted for her.

London jerked away from him. "Don't touch me."

Lynch smacked her across the face with his gun, causing a deep gash to appear on her cheek, and blood flowed freely onto the hotel floor.

"Ms. London!" Jada cried.

Lynch called out to Peanut, "Keep that brat quiet before I shut her up myself."

"Jada, it's okay, sweetheart. Everything's going to be okay." London looked the little girl directly in her eyes and she could see the fear in Jada's pupils. She wanted nothing more than to keep Kalil's daughter safe. "Why don't you let her go? I'll come with you. Just leave her alone. She has nothing to do with this."

Lynch pulled London out of the hotel room and Peanut pulled Jada and followed closely behind. Lynch whispered in London's ears as he led her through the hotel lobby and out the door, "If you say one word, my man is gon' murder the little girl."

He hit the button on his keys to pop the trunk and then forcefully stuffed London inside.

"Wait," she protested.

Her cries were ignored as they folded Jada up and stuffed her in next to London. They slammed the trunk, leaving London and Jada in the dark, cramped space.

"I want my daddy," Jada whispered.

From the sound of her voice, London could tell that she was crying. "Me too, sweetheart, me too," she said as she held on to Jada's hand tightly and closed her eyes. She prayed to God that this was a bad dream and that, when she opened her eyes, everything would be okay.

Chapter Twelve

Breaking news! We have live coverage of a high-speed chase happening right at this very moment. The authorities say that the chase has been in progress for over an hour and that the driver is holding nothing back!

Kalil watched the television and couldn't believe his eyes. June was on CNN, driving like a madman, trying to elude the cops. He watched as the white Lexus maneuvered in and out of lanes going at least 120 miles per hour. The sight of June's car made Kalil's jaws clench and fist ball up. Just hours earlier, he was looking down the barrel of June's gun, thinking his life was about to come to an end.

"Yo, Quinn, look at this shit!" Kalil yelled, his eyes glued to the fiasco. Kalil began to think about how he could have been in right alongside June in the high-speed chase. Thinking about it, he was sort of glad that June pulled that stunt. If he hadn't tried to kill Kalil, he would've been in the car with him.

Quinn entered the living room and saw the chase happening live and in living color. "Is that—"

Kalil cut Quinn off mid-sentence. "Yeah, that's that bitch-ass nigga."

They just stared at the television set and watched the drama unfold. June's Lexus caught a flat and began to fishtail, causing the vehicle to lose all control. The helicopter caught the whole chase from a bird's-eye view.

Just before June could gain control of the car, the inevitable happened and the chase was over. His car crashed into the back of a semitruck, causing him to spin around wildly, forcefully slamming his car into the guardrails alongside the highway.

BOOM!

The car instantly burst into gigantic flames, sending debris flying everywhere. The wild accident caused a domino effect, and cars began to spin crazily, causing a massive pileup. It was complete pandemonium unfolding live on CNN.

"Damn!" Quinn yelled as he watched it as if it was a high-packed action movie.

Almost instantly, Kalil and Quinn began to smile. It was sort of a guilty pleasure to see that June's karma had caught up with him so quickly.

"Karma's a bitch." Kalil turned off the TV and began to rub his bandaged chest. The spots where the gunshots hit were badly bruised and sore. But Kalil would take the bruises over holes anyway. "Yo, Quinn, if you didn't put the doubt in my head, I would be dead right now." Kalil thought about how he'd vested up just before the setup.

"I knew something was funny about the nigga. I just had a gut feeling. That's why I followed you there." Quinn slapped hands with his cousin.

"That's one less thing I have to worry about now. He should be glad I didn't catch up with him. I had something for him." Kalil sat on the couch and thought about his next task—telling Hova he had nothing for him. "Man, I owe Hova dope or money, and I have neither."

"What you going to do?" Quinn asked, ready for whatever.

"I'm going to see him."

Hova sat at his office desk that overlooked Club Heaven and smoked his Cuban cigar. His insides were boiling, thinking about his wife cheating with another man. What made him even more enraged was the fact that he knew her lover.

"I'm going to make that motherfucker pay. Both of them! I'm Hova, the be-all and end-all. I'm the god of this city. Who runs this? Me, that's who!" He slammed his fist into his desk. His usually pale white face was now bloodshot red. He ran his fingers through his short blond hair and aggressively pulled off his white Armani blazer, exposing his muscular physique.

A few of Hova's disciples watched as he grew angrier by the second. They knew how bad his temper was, so they remained silent and let him vent his frustrations. Hova had already put a hit on London and was eagerly awaiting the phone call to confirm her death. He had other plans for Kalil. He wanted to handle him personally. His manhood wouldn't allow Kalil to get away with having his wife behind his back.

Hova put out his cigar and ran his fingers through his hair, trying to regain his composure. The sound of his phone ringing filled the air.

"Speak!" Hova said as he picked up the phone. He got the information from the other end of the phone and smiled as he was receiving the news. Lynch and Peanut had London in their custody. Hova smiled as Lynch told him that they had a bonus: Jada, Kalil's daughter.

"Wait until I give the word and then do them both!" Hova didn't ask how old the child was before giving the order, and he didn't really care. He just wanted Kalil and London to suffer severely for the adulterous acts they had committed against him. His obsession with being "Hova the God" showed as he coldheartedly ordered the death of London and Jada.

Quinn looked over at Kalil in the passenger seat. "Are you sure you don't want me to go in there with you?"

Kalil held his aching chest and grimaced. "Nah, I'm good. I don't want to get you wrapped up in all of this shit. I have to handle this situation on my own."

"You sure?"

"Yeah, I'm good. If anything happens to me, just make sure Jada is all right," Kalil said as he opened the door.

"Fuck that! If you're not out in ten minutes, I'm coming in blasting, son." Quinn cocked his pistol and looked at his cousin.

Kalil reached in his cousin's car and slapped hands with him, realizing that he had a real comrade on his team. Then he walked up to the club, preparing to confront Hova.

***

Peanut's conscience came into play as he heard the muffled cries of the woman and child who rode in the trunk. He looked over at Lynch and got sick to the stomach at the fact that Lynch had no remorse for what was about to go down.

Lynch puffed on a blunt as he bobbed his head to the music. He turned up the stereo to drown out the kicks and screams of Jada and London.

Peanut shook his head from side to side with guilt as he thought about his role in the whole matter. "This shit ain't right, man." Peanut continued to shake his head.

"Look, man, I don't need you bitchin' up on me right now, Nut. Hova gave us a job to do, and I'm going to do it."

"This shit ain't right, Lynch. That's a kid back there, fam!" Peanut grew a disgusted look on his face.

They pulled up to the abandoned house that Hova owned and hopped out the car. Peanut was the first to get to the trunk. He took a deep breath and hit the trunk button, causing it to pop open. When he saw London and Jada tied up with duct tape over their mouths, he instantly become overridden with guilt.

Before he could even say anything, Lynch came over and forcefully snatched London out of the trunk and dragged her to the back-door entrance.

"Grab the kid!" he yelled, as he struggled with a kicking and squirming London.

Peanut reached for Jada, who jumped at his touch. He saw the fear in the young girl's teary eyes. He carefully picked her up and assured her, "I'm not going to hurt you." It hurt his heart, knowing that he would eventually have to kill her.

Kalil walked into the empty club and took a glance around. The club was a totally different scene in the daytime. He saw Hova's top-floor office and knew that he was playing with fire by coming back empty-handed. He was willing to get Hova's money back for him. He just needed some time to get back in the streets and make some moves. Kalil made his way up the stairs and to Hova's office door.

Hova yelled on his cell phone, "What the fuck do you mean? Those motherfuckers are going to pay. No Italians are going to muscle me. I'm Hova!"

The Italians and Hova had been in a turf war for a few months, and they'd given him an ultimatum: Give them a cut of the drug profit or "vest up."

He hung up the phone angrily. He wasn't worried about the Italians attempting to strong-arm him. He had other things on his mind, like making Kalil and London suffer.

One of the disciples said to Hova, "Hov, what do you wanna do about the Italians? If we move on them now, they're going to expect it."

Hova decided that he'd fall back to avoid walking into a trap. "We're going to lay low for a while, rock 'em to sleep, and then I'm going to bring the heat to those slick-haired bastards." Hova's reputation for retaliation was infamous, and he knew that if he sent any of his soldiers over to the Italians, he would only be sending them into a death trap. The Italians wanted a war and were waiting on him to make a move.

Tears streamed down London's face as she looked over at Jada, who had cried herself to sleep. London frantically looked around the damp basement they were in, and the smell of mildew and dampness nearly made her gag. Duct tape covered Jada's mouth, and her hands were tied as she slumped against the wall with dried-up tear stains on her cheek.

London squirmed, trying to free herself, but it was no use. The ropes were tightly knotted and there was no escaping. She knew that Lynch was Hova's head hit man and that he had no respect for human life whatsoever. Hova had told London stories about Lynch's murder game and how he just didn't give a fuck.

London began to regret creeping with Kalil at this point. She not only put her life at jeopardy, but now a little girl was in the midst of the chaos. London cried a river while the anticipation built. She knew that the men were just waiting on a call for Hova to end their lives. *Please, God, please spare Jada's life. She doesn't deserve this, she doesn't,* London thought to herself while guilt overwhelmed her.

At that moment, she heard the wooden stairs creaking. Someone was coming down. A man's silhouette appeared and the smell of his strong cologne filled the room. London scooted to the corner where Jada was and tried to shield her body. At this point, her only thought was to protect Jada. She saw that the man was Lynch and the fear factor set in. The look in his eyes was that of a madman, and London knew that her life was on a countdown.

Lynch slowly walked over to London with more than murder on his mind. He always envied Hova for having such a beautiful wife. He couldn't see how a white man got such a gorgeous woman as

London. Every time he would see her, he would dream about how good sex with her would be. He was finally about to make his dreams come true.

Lynch just stared at her awkwardly, a devilish grin plastered on his face. London noticed the bulge growing in his Sean Jean sweatpants as he approached.

"London, you one bad bitch! Why do you fuck wit' that arrogant-ass white boy? I know he lacking what I'm packing." Lynch grabbed his erect rod and began to stroke it. The pure beauty of London had him mesmerized, and he envisioned himself stroking her from the back. The closer he got to London, the harder his manhood became.

Kalil took a deep breath—not out of fear, but out of frustration—before knocking on Hova's door. He was ready to leave the game alone, but June's backstabbing set him back in his plans. He knew to repay Hova the money he would have to become the Kalil of the old. The hustler.

Knock, knock, knock! He lightly tapped the door as he rubbed his sore chest and waited for a response.

One of the disciples answered the door, and when he saw Kalil's face it was as if he saw a ghost. The disciple just stood there, not knowing what to say. Hova was just talking about what was going to happen when he found Kalil and there he was in the flesh. *This mu'fucka got balls.*

"What the fuck is yo' problem? Are you going to let me in or just stand there?" Kalil looked the man up and down. He had a rough day and wasn't trying to fuck around.

The disciple didn't say anything. He just smiled and stepped to the side to feed Kalil to the dogs.

Kalil stepped past the man and saw the back of Hova's oversized leather chair.

Hova's back was turned toward Kalil as he stared out of his glass window that overlooked the club. The smoke from his Cuban cigar danced into the air, letting Kalil know Hova was sitting there.

Kalil felt the tension in the room as everyone ceased the conversation when he entered. There were about three disciples scattered throughout the oversized luxury office. Kalil grew suspicious and began to study his surroundings. *Do they already know that I don't have the money? Everybody in this joint ice-grilling me and shit. These mu'fuckas gon' fuck around and get fucked up today. What the fuck is the problem, yo!* Kalil frowned up his face. He was fearless and returned every cold stare as he made his way to the front of Hova's desk. He cleared his throat in an attempt to grab Hova's attention.

Hova took his time in responding. Moments later he swung his chair around so that he was facing Kalil. "Kalil, one of my most trusted associates," he said sarcastically. He took a deep pull of his cigar. "I've been waiting to see you. You're back a lot sooner than I expected." Hova was boiling inside, and it took all of the willpower he could muster to prevent him from reaching in his desk and filling Kalil's body with bullets.

"Yeah," Kalil said, standing firm, "I had a little problem, nah mean? I need a little more time to hit you back. My man tried to backdoor me." Kalil pulled up his shirt, exposing the circled bruises. He didn't want to come with excuses, because he was a man and stood on his own two. He was ready for whatever. Hova was going to have to give him more time, or just make a move.

Hova glanced around at his disciples, all ready to kill Kalil at his request.

Kalil followed Hova's eyes and noticed that every disciple had their hand on their gun. He looked at the disciples, some of whom used to work for him, and yelled, "What the fuck is the problem?"

"The problem is that you owe me three hundred and sixty grand, and I want my money." Hova put out his cigar and stared Kalil directly in the eyes.

"Hova, you know I'm good for it. I just need a while to bounce back. I've spent much more than that with you over the years. What? I ain't good for it?" Kalil put his hands up.

Hova sat back in his chair and slowly crossed his legs, disregarding Kalil's question. "Kalil, I love my wife." He picked up the picture of his wife that sat on his desk.

Kalil wasn't trying to get into a crazy conversation with Hova. *What the fuck? I don't give a fuck,* he thought, wanting to get back on subject. Kalil knew Hova liked to play mind games and he had bigger fish to fry. He wanted to get hit with more bricks so he could repay his debt and get enough paper to move away with his daughter and the woman of his dreams.

"Yeah, but like I was saying, I need you to hit me," Kalil said, cutting to the chase.

"Listen! I love my wife!" Hova said in a more harsh tone, his face turning apple red. He slowly turned around the picture of London, revealing his wife's identity to Kalil.

London squirmed and cringed as Lynch forced her legs open and began to eat her out, giving her rough and sloppy oral sex. She wanted to put up more of a fight, but Jada was next to her 'sleep and she didn't want to wake her and have the child witness the degrading act that was happening to her. Eventually London stopped squirming and let the tears flow as Lynch had his way with her.

When Lynch was fully erect and had gotten her "wound" wet to his satisfaction, he was ready to enter her. He stood up and began to unbutton his pants. He let his pants drop, and his uncircumcised penis hung from his boxers. He was about eleven inches long, and the sight alone terrified her. He bent down and ripped the duct tape from over her mouth. He wanted to hear her beg and scream, to heighten his experience.

"Please, please, stop!" London whispered between cries. She tried her hardest to plead with Lynch without waking Jada. And by the look of Lynch's erect, throbbing dick, she knew there was no stopping him.

"Shut up, bitch. You know you want it. Stop playin' yaself." Lynch stroked his penis and stared at London's neatly trimmed vagina. Earlier he had ripped off all her clothes, leaving her butt naked. The only thing she had on was the ropes.

London came to the realization that Lynch wasn't concerned with her cries for help and she knew she was about to get raped. She reluctantly opened her legs. "Please, just do it away from her, please," she begged as her dignity dropped to an all-time low.

Lynch disregarded her request and dropped to his knees, ready for entry.

The sound of the wooden stairs creaking could be heard, and Peanut came into view.

"What the fuck are you doing, fam?" Peanut rushed toward Lynch, grabbed him by the back of the neck, and pushed him off London. "Are you crazy, man?" Peanut looked at Lynch like he was insane. Peanut had been upstairs on the john and couldn't believe what was happening while he left them unattended.

Lynch inched back over to London, thinking only about a nut. "What's yo' fucking problem? You can have her next after me."

Peanut grabbed him again and pulled him off her, this time more forcefully. He already was feeling guilty for kidnapping Kalil's people, so he wasn't going to sit there and allow Lynch to rape a woman. He pulled out his gun and pointed it at Lynch. "Get the fuck off of her, you sick mu'fucka!" he yelled, cocking the hammer back on the gun.

Lynch screwed up his face in disbelief. "Oh, you gon' shoot me over this sheisty bitch? She's dead anyway. Why you buggin'?" Lynch pulled up his pants.

"No, nigga, *you* buggin'. It's a little girl right here, and you got yo' joint all hanging out about to rape a female!" Peanut was extremely upset at that point. Lynch totally disgusted him. He didn't know that Lynch had a twisted side to him.

All the commotion woke up Jada, and she began to squirm in an attempt to release herself from the ropes. All of a sudden, Peanut felt Lynch's fist hit him square in the eye, causing him to drop the gun.

Lynch followed up with another punch. "You pulled a strap out on me, lil' nigga? Better use it next time." Lynch hit Peanut again with an uppercut, causing him to land flat on his back.

London and Jada watched in terror as the scene unfolded.

While the two men wrestled for the gun, Lynch's phone rang, ceasing all movement. It was Hova.

Kalil looked at the picture of London and was at a loss for words. He couldn't believe it. He stared at a wedding picture of Hova and London, both of them in all white. He was totally shocked. He was having an affair with his man's wife. His trophy wife. *What the hell is going on? Hova is London's husband? I can't believe this. I can't fucking believe this, yo! Does he know?*

"Yeah, I know you're fucking my wife," Hova said, as if he could read Kalil's thoughts.

Kalil was speechless as he stared into the man's eyes across from him. All along, the monster that London was petrified of was the powerful white man the streets called Hova.

"Look, Hova, it's not even—"

Before Kalil could finish his statement, one of Hova's disciples hit him unexpectedly. And suddenly five guns were pointed at him.

Hova wanted to kill Kalil right then and there, but he wanted to torture him before he put him to sleep forever. "You know what . . . no explanation needed, Kalil. London is a beautiful woman, isn't she?" Hova stated calmly. He was comfortable in his plush leather chair as he sat back with his arms folded behind his head, glaring at Kalil. He sat up suddenly.

Silence filled the air as Kalil tried to prepare himself for the unexpected. He couldn't read the man who sat before him, but he knew he was in a bad position.

"You know what? I want you to hear something." Hova pushed the speaker button on his desk phone and dialed a number.

Kalil froze, knowing he was outnumbered. He grabbed his bleeding head and winced as he waited for the throbbing pain to subside.

"Hello," a man answered on the other end.

Hova coldly stared into Kalil's eyes. "Put the kid on the phone!"

As the words rolled off Hova's tongue, Kalil's heart began to race. He didn't want to believe that Hova was referring to Jada.

"Hello?" a shaky innocent voice said.

Kalil yelled, "Jada!" His knees became weak.

"Daddy! Help!"

"Don't worry, baby girl. Daddy is coming to get you, I promise!" Kalil yelled almost in tears. Although Kalil was as tough as they come, the sound of his daughter's frightened voice broke him down.

The sound of Jada's screaming for her father was in the background as Lynch came on the phone. "What do you want me to do with London?" he asked.

"I'll call you back in a couple hours." Hova hung up the phone. He got a bright idea. He had no intentions of letting London, Kalil, or the little girl live, but first he wanted Kalil to suffer.

"Let them go, mu'fucka! If anything happens to them. I'ma kill you myself!" Kalil yelled. He tried to lunge at Hova, but before he could reach him, the disciple restrained him and gave him a couple of blows to the midsection.

"You're not in the position to be making threats, homeboy." Hova laughed and lit his Cuban cigar. "We are about to play a little game. You see, you owe me a lot of money and you've been fucking my wife. I have a little problem with the Moretti family, and I need it handled. I'm giving you three hours to bring me back Frank Moretti's chain, or your daughter and that bitch are dead. I want Moretti dead! You either handle my business or have your daughter's blood on your hands," Hova said, knowing that he was sending Kalil into a death trap.

The Italians had just sparked a war with his organization and were expecting Hova to strike back. He figured this was a creative way of killing Kalil as well as retaliating without losing any of his soldiers.

Hova gave one of disciples a signal, and immediately the disciple gave Kalil his loaded gun. Kalil looked at the gun that rested in his hand and wanted so badly to use it on Hova, but he knew he had his daughter's life in his hands.

"You have three hours." Hova nonchalantly turned his back on Kalil and looked out the glass window that overlooked the club.

Kalil rushed out the club and into Quinn's car.

Quinn noticed the frantic look on Kalil's face and asked, "You all right?"

Kalil shook his head from side to side. "They got Jada."

"What?" Quinn asked in confusion.

"Hova got Jada and London. I'ma kill that mu'fucka!" Kalil cocked back the gun, and he gripped the pistol so tightly, his hand began to shake.

Quinn was trying to understand the situation, but first he had to calm Kalil down to get the information. "Hold on, fam! Calm down. Why did he take Jada before you even told him about the bricks? What's going on?"

"Hova has my daughter." Kalil put his face in his hands and shook his head in disbelief. "This ain't about the drugs. London is his wife. He found out about us, and he's playing some sort of game. He gave me three hours to hit Moretti, or he's going to kill them both," Kalil said in a desperate tone.

"Word? You fuckin' Hova's wife? Fuck was you thinking, Kalil?" Quinn couldn't believe that Kalil was getting ready to beef out with the king of New York over a woman. He shook his head in frustration. "Fuck, Kalil!"

"I ain't know! She never told me her husband's name. He wasn't my concern. Now Jada's life is on the line." Kalil's voice cracked from the pressure of the cries that he kept subdued in his throat. "What am I gon' do?"

"What he told you to do. We gon' get at them Italian mu'fuckas. We don't have a choice. We got to save your shorty. We done bodied plenty of niggas for less than that."

By the sounds of things, Quinn knew that the situation was deep. He took a deep breath and pulled his pistol from his waist. He sat the gun on his lap, and without saying anything, he said a million words.

Kalil knew that his cousin was ready to go all out for his family. "I'm gon' murder that mu'fucka if he hurts my daughter. Word to my mother, if one hair on her head is out of place." Kalil couldn't contain his anger as Quinn pulled away from the curb.

All conversation ceased as both men became lost in their own thoughts.

In a way, Kalil felt guilty for putting his daughter in harm's way. He did love London dearly, but now he was second-guessing his decision to get involved with a married woman. He and London deserved whatever was coming to them, but Jada was innocent in the situation. She didn't make the choice to get involved in the affair, she was pulled into it by association and was now reaping the consequences. *I have to get my daughter back. I can't let anything happen to my baby girl,* Kalil thought as he drove himself crazy with possibilities of how the situation could end.

As he rode shotgun through the city streets, he tried to shake the thoughts of Jada and London out of his mind. He knew that he would have to stay focused in order to pull off the impossible mission that Hova had sent him on. He closed his eyes, tried to calm his brain, and leaned his seat back as he prepared to face his old boss, Mr. Moretti. This was the beginning of the end, and nobody but God could save him now.

Chapter Thirteen

"Damn, Kalil, pick up the phone. You sure that Moretti is in there?" Quinn loaded his semiautomatic handgun and eyed the building suspiciously.

"Yeah. It's the same routine with these mu'fuckas, man. They in there." Kalil loaded his own weapon and took a deep breath to calm his nerves. *Every time I try to get out of the game, something pulls me back in. This shit is gon' be the death of me, but I refuse to let it be the death of Jada.*

Kalil and Quinn exited the car.

"Go around to the back." Kalil crept up on the trailer that sat in the middle of the construction site and peeked through the window.

Frank Moretti and two other men were sitting at a table playing dominos, laughing and having a good time. Kalil knew that they would be there every Friday night for their domino game. He noticed that each man was strapped. Two guns were also on the table as they socialized and laughed amongst each other.

Quinn pulled the ski mask over his face and gave his cousin a pound. "All right, fam. Be careful. Let's do this shit quick and easy."

Kalil also pulled his mask over his face and then cocked his banger. He crept again to the door and inconspicuously peeked into the trailer.

"Fuck!" he whispered. He crouched back against the trailer and shook his head in disbelief. He still couldn't believe he had gotten involved with Hova's wife. He loved London dearly, but he would have approached his relationship with her completely differently if he'd known who she was. Because of his carelessness, London and his daughter's lives were threatened. *Get your mind right, baby,* Kalil thought to himself. *You can't save them if your head ain't right. Focus on what you doing and stick to the script.*

After reasoning with himself, Kalil knew there was no avoiding what he was about to do. He focused his attention on the Italian men inside of the trailer and listened closely as he overheard their conversation.

"That blond-hair faggot thinks he runs Manhattan. Fuck outta here! I'll run his ass uptown wit' the niggers. What type of man calls himself Hova anyways?" Frank Moretti puffed his cigar and smacked his domino onto the middle of the table.

The other men began to laugh at Moretti's comment and played their hands.

One man said, "I sent word through one of his goons that we want thirty percent like you asked."

"Yeah, if that faggot knows what's good for him, he'll break bread! I want in!" Frank Moretti grabbed his crotch and blew out two smoke circles.

"Hey, Paulie, did you pick up the dough from the niggers uptown?" Moretti remembered it was that time of the month for his pickups. Extortion was the Moretti family's main hustle, and they had a hand in everyone's pot. Everyone except for Hova's.

"Yeah, I picked up fifty large this morning from the niggers in Harlem. They're making a pretty penny off those blocks. Maybe we need to demand a bigger percentage."

Frank shook his head. "Nah, it's best to just play fair for now. What did you do with the money?"

Paulie threw his head in the direction of the back room. "It's in the safe in the back."

That statement was music to Kalil's ears. *I might as well get that cash too,* he thought as he prepared to handle his business. He could use the cash, so he could kill two birds with one stone on this hit. Kalil gripped his gun tighter as he thought about the lives that were on the line. He knew that he was walking into a situation where the odds were against him, but he didn't care at that point. His only concern was killing Moretti.

Tap, tap, tap!

Kalil heard his cue. Quinn was knocking on the back door to focus all of their attention toward the back. Kalil peeked in and watched as all their heads turned toward the back door.

"Who the fuck is that?" Moretti whispered.

His goons put their hands on their guns and stood up. Once they headed to the back, leaving Moretti in the front room alone, Kalil swiftly opened the door and crept up behind him while his head was turned.

Before Moretti could even react, Kalil's pressed his pistol to the back of his head. "You know what time it is! Lay the fuck down or I'ma pop off," Kalil whispered menacingly in his ear as he lightly jabbed the back of Moretti's head with the gun.

"Fuck!" Moretti mumbled as he did what he was told.

By the time Moretti hit the floor, his goons were returning to the front. They didn't even notice the masked man until it was too late. They had already put their pistols on their waistlines.

"Put yo' hands the fuck up, or I'ma pop this mu'fucka!' Kalil poked the gun to the back of Moretti's head.

Paulie reached for his pistol, but before he even had it aimed well, Kalil fired a shot that went through the bottom of the trailer, inches away from Moretti's head.

"Goddammit! Son of a bitch!" Moretti yelled out in fear as his body involuntarily jumped from the sound of the gunshot.

"Next time I won't miss. You better tell your goons to fall back," Kalil told Moretti.

"Do what he says," Moretti mumbled.

The henchmen instantly put up their hands for fear that their boss would get shot. That's when Quinn came from the back entrance and pulled the guns off the goons. What they thought was a bird tapping on the window was the beginning stages of an ambush.

"Tie their asses up," Kalil said as he pressed the gun to the back of Moretti's head.

Quinn hit one of the goons, causing him to collapse to the floor. He hit the other man soon after and tied them both up with the rope he had brought.

Kalil put his knee into Moretti's back. "Yo, where the dough at?"

"Do you know who the fuck you are fuckin' with?" Moretti had a slight grin on his face.

His smug arrogance was trying Kalil's patience. "Shut the fuck up!" Kalil hit him with a forceful blow to the back of the head with his gun. "I'ma ask you one more time—Where is the dough?"

Blood leaked out of Moretti's head as he winced in pain. "Fuck you!" he yelled.

Without hesitation, Kalil pointed his gun at one of the goons and let a round off into his head. It was all or nothing for Kalil, and he wasn't playing any games.

Moretti yelled, "Paulie!" as he watched his cousin gasp for air and hold his bloody wound.

"You bastard motherfucker! If I live through this I am going to hunt you down. You don't know who you are fucking with!"

Moretti spewed the words at him as if he was throwing fire, but it didn't make a difference to Kalil. He was already beefing with Hova, so he had no fear of starting beef with the Italians. At that point he didn't care about himself. He was only thinking of saving Jada and, if he could, saving London as well.

"Where the stash?" Kalil yelled again.

"It's in the back. The combo is seven, thirty-one, twenty-three," one of the other men admitted, knowing that Moretti would die before he gave in.

Kalil nodded his head at Quinn, signaling him to get the cash, and Quinn hurried to the back while Kalil kept an eye on the two men.

Moretti was furious; he didn't care if he lived or died at that point. "You better kill me! I'm going to find you and gut you like a fuckin' fish!" he yelled.

Just then, Quinn came out of the back with four brown paper bags full of money. "Jackpot!" he said as he entered the room.

Kalil knew it was time to do what he came to do. He put the gun to Moretti's head and pulled the trigger.

Boom!

"Hova sends his best regards," Kalil said loud enough so the other men could hear him clearly. He wanted to let it be known that the hit was from Hova, so eventually the Moretti family would retaliate on him. Kalil's adrenaline began to pump as he saw Moretti's body lying there lifeless, but he knew it had to be done. He had to get London and Jada out of the bad situation.

He reached down and violently snatched the thin gold necklace from Moretti's neck. It was nothing extravagant, just a fourteen-karat gold chain with a small gold cross attached to it. It was sacred to Moretti and had been given to him when he was a young boy.

Kalil stuffed the chain into his pocket and left the scene, Quinn following close behind. Kalil purposely left the two men alive to be messengers. He was sure that Hova would get his, one way or another.

Chapter Fourteen

The room was tense and the only sound that could be heard was Jada as she whimpered in London's lap.

"Shut that lil' bitch up, man! She's getting on my fuckin' nerves." Lynch eyed Jada cruelly. "Fuck is taking Hova so long to call us back? I'm ready to dead these bitches and get the fuck out of here."

Peanut flipped the face up to his cell phone to see if he had any missed calls. "Just shut the fuck up and wait for the call, Lynch." He was hoping that Kalil would hit him back, because time was running out and there was only so much he could do before the inevitable occurred.

London trembled at the thought of her fate. *I was so close to freedom,* she thought as a tear slid down her ashen face. She'd never imagined that her life would end so violently. She didn't want Jada to go through the pain that she knew was waiting for them both. "Ssh. Just go to sleep, sweetheart. When you wake up, it'll all be over," she said, trying to soothe the young girl's soul.

At that point she knew that she was going to die. There was no way that she could cheat death when dealing with someone as cold as her husband. The only thing that she could do was pray to God to take her quickly, but in her heart she knew that Lynch would enjoy each and every minute of her torture. He would prolong her life until he was tired of watching her breathe and would then put her to rest as if she were a stray dog.

London was hoping that they would spare Jada, and if they didn't, she could only hope that she wouldn't suffer much pain.

"I want my daddy," Jada moaned.

"I know, I know," London replied.

"Yo, shut the fuck up!" Lynch couldn't wait to put his hostages out of their misery.

Peanut knew that in less than an hour Hova was going to order the murder of Kalil's daughter and there was nothing he could do to stop it. "I'll be back, fam. I got to piss like a mu'fucka." He grabbed his crotch and trotted up the basement steps, skipping two at a time. Once he was out of ear's reach, he pulled out his cell phone in one last desperate attempt and dialed Kalil's number. *Damn, Kalil, pick up the phone.*

***

Quinn sat in his apartment feverishly counting the money that they'd just lifted from the Italians while Kalil paced nervously in front of him. The kitchen table was covered with cash, bills of all different denominations. It was evident that it was dirty money because all of the bills were crumpled and gritty. Anyone who knew the dope game could tell that the money had been passed from hand to hand countless times.

"Man, stop pacing back and forth like that. You fucking up my count." Quinn was under enough pressure just knowing that his little niece was being held hostage and Kalil was spazzing out, making the situation more stressful.

Kalil walked the same back-and-forth pattern that he'd been doing for the last half hour. "How much is it, fam? Please tell me it's enough to help me get my shorty back."

"It's a start." Quinn rose from the table and shoveled the money back into the duffel bag. "It's around seventy stacks." He handed the bag to Kalil.

"That ain't even half of what I owe." Kalil felt the vibration of his phone against his hip. He looked at it before answering. "I don't got time for you right now, Nut," he whispered. He sent Peanut to voice mail and placed his phone back in its clip.

Just then his phone vibrated again and he picked it up, this time recognizing Hova's number. He hit the button to connect the call and placed the phone to his ear. He waited for Hova to speak first.

"Tick, tock, Kalil. You're running out of time," Hova stated, laughter in his voice.

The sound of Hova's voice infuriated Kalil. Hova really was a sick man. He was enjoying the torture that he was putting Kalil through.

"I did what you asked me to do. Moretti is a done deal. Now give me back my daughter!" Kalil shouted into the phone, his jaw locked from the rage he was feeling.

"You might want to change your tone and remember who you are speaking with. I have something that you are trying to get back. Bring me Moretti's chain and maybe, just maybe, I'll let Daddy see his little girl again."

"I got the chain, yo. Just don't hurt her." Kalil hated being powerless, but he knew that there was nothing that he could do at the moment. He had to go along with Hova's antics if he wanted to get his child back. His heart beat so loudly in his chest that it felt like a thousand slaves were trying to break out to freedom. His pride as a man and as a father was being tested and he knew that he couldn't let Hova get away with this. *This mu'fucka gon' see me. If it's the last thing I do, I'm gon' get Jada back, and once she's safe, I'm gon' make sure that I'm the last thing Hova sees before he meets his maker.*

"Tick tock, Kalil," Hova taunted one last time before hanging up the phone.

Kalil threw his phone against the wall and rushed out of the room and into Quinn's room.

Quinn immediately noticed the change in his cousin's temperature. "Kalil, what did he say?" He could see the heat in Kalil's eyes and he already knew what time it was.

Kalil didn't respond. He went into the top of the closet and pulled out the pistols that they both kept hidden. He put a 9 mm pistol in his waistline as his face turned red and tears gathered in his eyes. Then he pulled out a .45, popped the clip loudly into place, and then tossed a .357 Ruger at Quinn. "It's time to stop playing with this mu'fucka. He got my fucking daughter tied the fuck up somewhere. I'm about to put this nigga in the ground."

Kalil pushed one of Hova's disciples out of his personal space as he entered the room. "Fuck is you doing, nigga? Get your fucking hands off me."

The disciple wanted to boss up but he could tell by the look on Kalil's face that it was in his best interests to get out of the way.

Quinn, meanwhile, kept his hand tucked discreetly in his hoodie as he gripped his pistol and counted the number of disciples around the room. He knew they were clearly outnumbered, but he was ready to put in work for his cousin.

Hova was still seated in his chair, his feet resting on the long conference table.

Kalil slid the necklace across the table and placed the duffel bag in front of him. "I did what you asked me to. Here's a portion of the money I owe you. You know I'm good for the rest. Just give me my daughter, and I swear you'll see every single penny."

Hova smiled and looked down at his Presidential Rolex. "You made it in the nick of time."

"Where's Jada?" Kalil asked through clenched teeth. He was trying to control his anger because he knew that he didn't have room for error. One wrong move could mean the death of his daughter, and he was fighting desperately to keep her alive.

"Jada? That's your daughter's name?" Hova stared intently at Kalil. "Tell me, Kalil, I'm very curious to know—it's obvious that you love your child—why would you put her life in danger by fucking my wife? You had to know that your little secret would eventually come out. What is it you black motherfuckers say?" Hova snapped his fingers repeatedly as he tried to jog his memory. "All things done in the dark will eventually come to light. Yeah, that's it."

Kalil didn't feel the need to explain himself. "I just want my daughter. Let her go. Let London go. This is between us," Kalil stated. "I made the choice to fuck with London. I should be the one to pay the consequences."

"This broke black motherfucker wants to call the shots." Hova chuckled lightly. He sat up and folded his hands across the conference table.

As silence filled the room, Quinn shifted in his stance from anticipation. He could feel his hands clamming up as he waited to see how the situation would play out.

Peanut checked the time on his phone and noticed that it was almost time to get down to business. He knew what was supposed to go down but in his heart he couldn't betray his mans like that. By going against the grain he knew that he would have to man up and come out blazing, but he couldn't find it in him to be a part of Kalil's setup.

Lynch yelled from the basement, "Fuck you doing up there, nigga? It's almost time. Hova gon' be calling any minute!"

Peanut nodded his head. He removed the .380 pistol from his waistline and ensured that it was loaded before he put it back in his pants. He walked down the steps, keeping his hand discreetly on his pistol for reassurance. He watched as Lynch pulled London to her feet, violently pulling her up by her hair as he made her stand in front of him.

London found herself staring down the dark barrel of a gun as her tears flowed freely. She looked back at Jada, who was asleep against the wall.

"You should've let me hit this pussy. Maybe it wouldn't have had to come to this," Lynch sneered as he pulled the hammer back on his gun.

London closed her eyes and felt the tears burn her eyes. Not wanting to give Lynch the satisfaction of witnessing her tears, she inhaled deeply and prepared herself for the darkness to come. Her mind drifted to Kalil. She wanted him to be the last thing that she thought of before she was rocked into a forced sleep.

Boom!

"Aww!" London screamed as blood and brains from Lynch's head splattered all over her face.

"Ms. London!" Jada yelled.

A hysterical London ran over to Jada and put her hands over the young child's eyes.

"Ms. London!"

London looked up in horror at Peanut as he aimed. He put one more hollow in Lynch's dead body just for the hell of it.

She pulled Jada close. She was sure that they were next.

Just as Peanut began to approach them a ringing phone interrupted his stride. The ringing was coming from Lynch's pants pocket. He searched the dead body frantically, knowing that missing Hova's call would raise a red flag.

London eyed the body on the floor as blood began to creep her way. She nodded her head and then leaned into Jada and said, "Ssh. Everything is going to be okay." She put her hand over Jada's mouth and then kissed the top of her head.

Peanut answered the phone. "Hello?"

"Why did it take you so long to answer the phone?"

"We had to find the damn phone," Peanut explained. "This dumb nigga left the shit upstairs."

"It's time," Hova told him.

"All you got to do is give me the go-ahead."

"Kill them both. I want Kalil to hear them die."

Boom! Boom!

Screams erupted through the basement as the gunshots rang out. Once the loud noise ceased, Peanut disconnected the call, shaking his head from side to side in regret.

Chapter Fifteen

Peanut sped toward Club Heaven in heavy desperation. He knew that Kalil was in a bad predicament and was trying to get there before it was too late. He realized that he owed Kalil too much to not help him. *I can't even believe I was about to go through with it! I gotta help my mans,* Peanut thought as he weaved in and out of traffic, trying to get there as soon as possible.

Kalil had practically taught him how to become a man, and he finally came to his senses. He just hoped it wasn't too late. He'd assured London and Jada that they would be okay and took them to his apartment as a safe haven. But London refused the offer and wanted to go with Peanut. Peanut didn't have time to argue with her, and let them tag along as he raced to the club at 100 mph with two pistols in his lap. Now his only concern was to help Kalil. He knew that Hova was going to have him killed.

***

Kalil cried like a baby as the men held him down while he was on his knees. He then looked over at Quinn's lifeless body that laid in his own blood. Hova had ordered one of the disciples to kill Kalil's cousin right before his eyes. He wanted Kalil to suffer in the worst way.

"Quinn," Kalil called out, hoping that his cousin would answer, but it was too late. He was gone. Kalil had heard the death of his baby girl because Hova had Peanut on speakerphone.

"Jada, Jada, my baby girl, I'm sorry," Kalil whispered as he bawled. Hova had brutally ordered the hit and he'd lost his daughter and his only true love, London. It was an out-of-body experience and Kalil's world came crumbling down.

Kalil was severely beaten. The disciples had a field day with him, at the discretion of Hova. The blood dripped from his mouth, and his left eye was swollen nearly shut. Two of the disciples restrained him as he used the last bit of energy he had trying to get to Hova, who nonchalantly sat at the edge of his desk smoking his cigar.

"Jada! Jada!" he yelled at the top of his lungs as he thought about what had happened a half an hour earlier. Kalil was on his knees facing Hova.

The twenty-minute beatdown he had just received didn't add up to a fraction of the pain he'd

felt when Hova said the words, "Kill them both."
He wanted to kill Hova with his bare hands so
badly, but he couldn't get to him. His disciples
had beaten him so badly, he could barely move.

One of the disciples held Kalil's face up so that
he was staring directly at Hova. Every time Hova
looked at Kalil he grew angrier. The thought of
his wife with another man was too much for him
to bear.

"Why! Why did you touch the forbidden fruit?
I'm Hova! Now I'm going to reunite you with
that bitch and your kid. What's my name?" Hova
screamed as he reached into his desk and pulled
out a chrome .38 pistol. He pressed the gun to
Kalil's forehead.

Kalil stared directly into Hova's eyes, showing
no sign of fear whatsoever. He was ready to die.
He had nothing to live for anymore. He was
ready to meet his maker. He tried to mumble
something, but he was so beaten and exhausted,
it barely came out.

"What's that?" Hova said, smiling. He knew
that he had totally stripped Kalil's manhood
away from him. He wanted to hear Kalil call him
Hova before he killed him. "Huh? What's that?"
Hova kneeled down to hear Kalil better.

"Fuck you! See you in hell, mu'fucka!" Kali
whispered weakly as he spat in Hova's face.

Outraged, Hova immediately wiped the bloody spit from his eyes. He couldn't wait any longer, he pressed the gun to Kalil's head.

Boom!

The sound of glass shattering startled Hova before he could kill Kalil. Dozens of bullets came flying through the glass. Everyone dropped to the floor and reached for their weapons as hollow-tips rained. The Moretti crew had come in the club, guns blazing. The sound of assault rifles and machine guns filled the air, and the club became an instant war zone.

While the disciples returned fire, Kalil scuffled his way behind Hova's desk for cover.

"Stop them from coming up the stairs!" Hova commanded. He reloaded his clip and returned fire.

Half of the disciples ran out of the office and headed down the wraparound stairs. Before they could even reach the bottom, the Italians loaded them up with bullets, dropping them one by one.

Kalil peeked out and watched as all the disciples crowded around Hova, as if they were a human shield, and exchanged bullets with the Italians on the main floor of the club. Bullets flew for what seemed like forever.

Kalil watched as they began to kill each other one by one. Bodies were getting filled with bullets and jerking left to right. Everyone in the room was on some real gangster shit. A roomful of Scarfaces, for real.

The disciples were down to three members, and the Italians had two henchmen left. Hova bitched up and followed his disciples as they tried to shoot his boss out to safety. They then went on the main floor and traded shots with the remaining Italians.

When the shooting finally stopped, Kalil came from under the desk. He looked down on the main floor and noticed that it was covered with dead bodies and blood. The sight was a gruesome one. No one was left standing. Kalil hadn't seen so many dead bodies in his life. It looked more like a horror movie than a scene from real life.

Peanut's black Ford Expedition skidded into the club's parking lot, nearly doing a doughnut. He threw the truck in park and gave London one of his guns. "If anyone comes to the car, shoot first and ask questions later." He quickly hopped out of the car and headed into the building.

London tried to ask, "But what if—" but Peanut had already exited the car. She looked at Jada and assured her that she was going to see her father very soon. All she could do was wait.

***

Kalil crept down the stairs in search of Hova. He prayed that he wasn't dead, because he wanted to kill him personally. Tears flowed down his cheek, and his limbs trembled as he frantically searched the room. He stepped over the dead bodies scattered across the dance floor. He couldn't believe his eyes. The Italians and the disciples had managed to kill off each other.

Kalil screamed, "Hova! Come out, you bitch-ass mu'fucka!" He stood in the middle of the room, his fist clenched. He knew Hova was hiding somewhere in the club, 'cause there was no sign of him. Kalil spotted a gun in one of the dead disciple's hands. He grabbed it with one thing on his mind—avenging Jada and London's death.

Hova hid underneath the liquor bar, his gun gripped tight. He only had one bullet left and began to think about his next move. He quickly peeked at the dance floor and watched as Kalil picked up a gun from one of the dead bodies. "Fuck!" he whispered to himself. He knew that a shoot-out was out of the question, especially with one bullet.

"Hova!"

Hova knew that after what he did to Jada, Kalil wasn't trying to talk. His hand began to shake uncontrollably. With all of his soldiers dead, he came to the realization that without the protection of his disciples, he was powerless.

Peanut entered the club and walked into what looked like a graveyard, dead bodies piled up one on top of the other throughout the main floor, the smell of death in the air. He scanned the floor, hoping not to see Kalil's body among the dead.

"Come on, Kalil, where you at?" Peanut whispered to himself. He looked up to the second floor at Hova's shattered office. Just as his eyes returned back to the main floor, he saw Kalil walking toward him, a weird glare in his eyes. Peanut instantly smiled and walked toward Kalil, throwing his hands up in relief. "Kalil, there you are. London and Jada are in—"

Before he could even finish his sentence, Kalil raised his gun and shot a bullet into his arm, causing him to drop his gun.

Kalil had spotted Peanut walking into the club and complete fury took over his body. Peanut had raised his hands and said something to him, but the only thing Kalil could hear was the two gunshots that rang through the speakerphone earlier.

"Aghh!" Peanut yelled in agony as he hit the floor and grabbed his wounded arm. *What the fuck is he doing?* Peanut thought as the burning sensation emerged. He couldn't understand why Kalil had bust at him.

Kali walked over and hovered over him with his gun pointed directly at his head.

"Kalil, what you doing, fam?"

"I heard you. I fucking heard you kill my baby!" Kalil said, tears streaming down his face.

Before Peanut could tell him that he didn't kill them and that they were in the car, Kalil squeezed the trigger.

Boom!

One bullet through the forehead killed Peanut on contact. Kalil then emptied the entire clip into his body, filling him with holes. Letting off all the shots were like instant therapy for Kalil. He didn't care anymore.

After he found Hova, he promised himself he would reunite himself with Jada and London in death. "I used to have love for you, lil' man. I hate you! I hate you! You took all that I had," Kalil said, shooting round after round into Peanut's lifeless body.

Peanut's eyes stared into space as Kalil stood over him still pulling the trigger although the gun was empty.

Kalil thought about an infamous hood quote: *They say if you die with your eyes open, you deserved it.* He looked around knowing that Hova was somewhere in the large club. He kept his eyes on the door and knew that he hadn't escaped. Now the only thing he had to do was find him.

London began to get antsy as she heard the gunshots come from the inside of the club. "Oh my God," she whispered as she put her hand over her mouth. She only could hope that the gunshots she'd heard weren't for Kalil. At that point she didn't know if he was dead or alive, and it was eating her up inside. She felt like it was all her fault. She knew that she was playing with fire by creeping around with him, but love blinded her judgment.

"Jada, baby, let's play a game. I want you to hide in the backseat until I get back, okay?" London said as she unskillfully picked up Peanut's gun.

"Okay, Miss London," Jada said naively.

London watched as Jada climbed over the seats and into the back. She didn't know what she was about to do, but she knew she had to do something. She clenched the pistol and exited the truck. *Hova is insane. I hope Kalil is okay. This bullshit is all my fault.*

Hova's chest felt like he had a baboon on the inside trying to get out. His heart was beating so hard and fast, it was nearly unbearable. He had peeked over the bar and watched as Kalil emptied the whole clip into Peanut. If he could do that to his former protégé, Hova couldn't even fathom what he was planning for him.

He took out the clip and checked to see if he had any more bullets, as if he didn't already know. Fuck! He knew he had two options: take Kalil out with one bullet, or hide like a bitch, hoping that Kalil wouldn't find him. He had no idea that option three was getting ready to walk through the door.

London frantically snatched open the entry door. She didn't know what she planned on doing to help, but she knew that she couldn't just sit in the car and do nothing while Kalil was inside fighting for his life.

Nothing could have prepared her for the carnage that she witnessed when she entered the main room of the club. Her mouth dropped in astonishment, and her stomach turned at the sight of all the blood that covered the dance floor. There was one man still standing, and his gun was aimed at the body of Peanut.

Oh my God, no. Peanut, she thought as she stood silent and motionless in the entryway. Her almond-shaped eyes widened in distress when she realized that the man standing before her was Kalil. "Kalil, what did you do?" she whispered loud enough for him to look her way.

London's voice was like sweet music to Kalil's ears. He thought he'd never hear it again. "London?" He looked back at Peanut, who had been like a little brother to him for many years. "Fuck did I do?" Kalil knelt down beside Peanut. "I thought he killed you. I thought he killed my daughter," Kalil tried to explain.

"You didn't know," London said softly.

Kalil was silent for a minute as he closed his eyes and said a quick prayer to God for Peanut's soul.

He stood to his feet, and just as he turned toward London, he saw Hova come out of the bar and approach her from behind.

"London, watch out!" He tried to warn her, but his words were not quick enough. Hova was already positioned behind her with a pistol to her head.

Kalil ran toward London, tripping over the dead bodies that lay scattered throughout the room. He tried to reach her, but Hova quickly halted him by aiming the gun in his direction.

"You can be Superman if you want to. I guarantee these bullets won't bounce off of you, though." Hova knew that he only had one bullet for one person, but he figured that he had room to bluff, now that he had London's life in his hands. The tables had quickly turned back in his favor. *I'm in control,* he thought to himself.

London screamed, "Kalil!" as she reached for him.

"You hear that, Kalil? The love of your life is calling for you." Hova stared Kalil down with hatred. "Now put down the fucking gun, unless you want me to splatter her brains on the fucking floor." He pressed the gun firmly against London's head.

"Aghh, Jake, please," she begged. "I'll do anything. Just please don't hurt him."

It was at that moment that Kalil realized that London loved him in the exact same way that he did her. Her only worry was for his safety, and for that he would always love her, even in his death. He knew that if London was still alive then so was Jada. They would be fine as long as they had each other. She was the type of woman that he wanted to raise Jada. The type of woman that he wanted Jada to be when she grew up. He trusted her with his daughter's life.

I'm willing to leave this earth today so that London and my daughter can live tomorrow, he thought to himself. He still had the gun gripped tightly in his hands, and tears flooded his eyes as he realized that his time in this world was about to come to an end.

"Put the gun down," Hova stated again.

"You want to be a part of this game, Hova. Well, this is a game that is played among men. I need your word as a man that if I put down my gun you will let London go. You can do what you want with me, but let her walk out of this with her life."

"Kalil, no!" London screamed. "Kalil, I love you." She began to buck against Hova so that she could get to Kalil.

"Bitch, shut up!"

"Do I have your word?" Kalil waited for Hova's response.

"You have my word," Hova said, knowing good well he would never let London see another sunset.

Kalil put the gun down on the ground in front of him and raised both hands slowly.

Hova laughed wholeheartedly. "You really are as dumb as you look. Sucker for love! You're a pussy! You really think I'm gonna let this cheating bitch get out of here alive?"

"Jake, please . . . I'll do anything," she whispered.

"You hear that, Kalil. This bitch will do anything. Let's think . . . what should I make her do?"

Kalil could tell from the sinister tone in Hova's voice that he had something in store for her. "I love you, London," he said.

London's head hung low in defeat.

"Look at me," Kalil told her.

She raised her head and met his gaze.

"I love you, ma," he repeated, accepting the fact that his life was about to end.

"I love you," she answered, not caring that her husband could hear her. She knew that Kalil was saying good-bye to her. "I'll always love you."

London's words must have been the straw that broke the camel's back because Hova pulled the trigger, sending his last bullet into her back. Her face contorted in pain as the hollow-point ripped through her insides, destroying the organs that sustained her life, and her limp body fell forward.

"No!" Kalil's voice came from the pit of his stomach and echoed through the entire club as he rushed toward Hova.

Hova didn't even get a chance to run. Kalil tackled him to the floor and rained punch after punch down on him. "Why!" he yelled in a voice that even he didn't recognize. Blinded by revenge, he beat Hova mercilessly. He hit Hova so hard that he could feel the bones in his hand breaking on impact, but he didn't care. He couldn't stop himself if he wanted to. "You took her away from me!" he roared.

The sound of Kalil connecting with Hova's head was sickening.

Whack! Whack! Whack! Whack!

Hova's Abercrombie-model features quickly became unrecognizable as Kalil brought the man closer and closer to death.

"Kalil," London muttered weakly.

Kalil turned around and saw London fighting to breathe. She was fighting for her life as her body shook on the floor. His anger instantly turned to concern as he scrambled on his knees to her side.

"London," he cried as he looked down at her. She was just as beautiful as the day she'd first entered his life. He rolled her onto her side and saw the hole in her chest and the huge puddle of blood that had formed underneath her. "Aghh," was the only sound that left his lips.

Kalil quickly lifted her body onto his lap. "London, don't leave me. Come on, ma, I need you."

He stroked her hair and looked her in the eyes.

"I'm dying, Kalil," she whispered.

"No, no, you're not, baby. Don't say that. You can't die on me. You still got to marry me. You still got to have my kids. London, just breathe for me!" he begged her as if she could stop what was happening.

"It's okay, Kal—" She stopped because it was getting hard for her to speak. She opened her mouth again. "You have given me so much. My life wasn't worth living until I met you. You showed me what love is, what it's like to be with a real man. If I had to do it all over again, I wouldn't change anything."

Kalil was falling to pieces right in front of her. He was supposed to protect her, and now the woman of his dreams was dying in his arms and it was all his fault.

"Remember what you told me when we first met."

Kalil was too stricken with grief to respond.

"You said that as long as you were in here"— she pointed to her heart—"then you would always be with me. It's true, Kalil. We'll always be together. I'll never leave you, even in death. Every time you feel the wind blow across your face, that will be me kissing you. Our love will never die, Kalil. It is too—" London coughed violently, causing blood to come out of the sides of her mouth. "It is too great," she finished weakly.

"London, don't talk like that, baby. You're going to be fine. You have to be with me. I can't do this. Come on, London, stay with me, ma."

"I can't, Kalil. I love you. I love you more than life. You saved me, Kalil, and I'll always be with you. Can you do me one favor?"

"Anything."

"Can you make sure that my tombstone reads with your last name?" she asked him. "I know we're not—"

Kalil put his finger to London's lips. "It doesn't matter. You are my wife. We don't need a man to confirm what God already knows. You're the only woman that I will ever give my last name to, I swear on my daughter's life."

London weakly grabbed Kalil's hand. "Just stay with me. Please don't leave my side until it's over," she said.

He nodded and leaned over to kiss her dying lips. It was the first time that he'd felt true heartbreak. He looked down into her eyes and could see that she was leaving the physical world and entering the spiritual.

"I'm right here, London," he whispered in her ear as he placed one hand on her chest. "I remember the first day I saw you. You were so beautiful, dancing on that stage. I knew that I needed to be with you. You were made for me. You've changed my life in so many ways, London, and I thank you for gracing me with your presence, even if only for a little while."

He felt London's grip loosen on his hand. She gasped lightly and, with a blank stare, said, "I'm always with you."

Kalil gently closed her eyes and cried like a newborn baby.

He heard the sounds of grunting from behind him. Realizing it was Hova, he lifted London off him and weakly walked over to the man who was writhing from the beating that he had received.

Kalil picked up Hova's gun, which lay at his feet. The same gun Hova had used to kill London. Kalil felt that he should send Hova to hell with the same gun. He got up, stood over Hova, and looked him directly in the eyes. He pulled the trigger, but of course the clip was empty.

"Freeze! Drop your weapon and put your hands where I can see them!"

Kalil didn't comply. He had to bring death to Hova. He couldn't let him live. Kalil attacked him, pistol-whipping him only for a short time before he was apprehended by the police.

Kalil felt a bullet rip through his leg as he fell to the ground. "Aghh!" he screamed in pain.

The bullets were followed by a parade of police batons pounding on his head and back.

As they carried Kalil out of the club, he could hear his daughter screaming for him.

"Daddy! Daddy! Wait, don't leave me!" Jada yelled as she hopped out of the car and ran toward him.

Kalil looked up to see his daughter crying. "Don't touch her! Don't you fucking touch her!" he yelled, jerking wildly in an attempt to free himself of the police restraints.

One of the officers yelled, "Listen! Listen! You need to calm down. Don't act a fool in front of your daughter. She's already traumatized enough. We'll make sure everything is okay with her."

Kalil's nostrils flared when he saw a police-woman escort Jada away from the club and into a police car. Jada was the only thing that he had left. He calmed down for the sake of his child and allowed the police to take him into custody, mouthing the words, "I love you," as the car pulled away.

It was the last time that he ever saw his daughter and the most tragic day of his life, one that would haunt him for the rest of his years.

Knut looked up to see his daughter crying.

"Don't touch her! Don't you fucking touch her," he yelled, futilely in an attempt to free himself of the police restraints.

One of the officers yelled, "Listen! Listen! You need to calm down. Don't lace about in front of your daughter. She's already traumatized enough. We'll make this by ... getting a ... with her."

Knut's nostrils flared when he saw a police woman escort ... la away from the club and into a police car. Kadi was the only thing that he had left. He carried much for the sake of his child and allowed the police to take him into custody, mouthing the words "I love you" as the car pulled away.

It was the last time that Knut saw his daughter ... and the next single day of his life, one that ... would haunt him for the rest of his years.

Epilogue

We're here to see Kalil Kelly," JaQuavis said as he and Ashley stood at the check-in desk at Rikers Island Penitentiary.

Ashley held the completed manuscript of Kalil's story in her hand and wanted him to be the first to read it. They'd worked nonstop on it for a whole week and completed it on the seventh day. The both of them were so involved in the story, it seemed as if they'd known Kalil their entire lives. Kalil told them his story so vividly that it was etched in both of their brains.

The guard who sat behind the desk looked at JaQuavis like he was crazy. "I'm sorry, but Mr. Kelly passed. One of the guards found him yesterday in his cell, dead. The poor fella hung himself."

"What?" JaQuavis said.

"That can't be right." Ashley put her hands on her hips in disbelief. "We just saw him a week ago." Her lips began to tremble in sorrow, and her eyes watered. Kalil had touched her with his story, and she couldn't believe he was dead.

"I don't know what to tell you, ma'am. He's gone." The guard tapped his pen against the desk.

The authors left out the prison in total disbelief. Of all their books, this particular one was closest to their heart. Kalil had taken them on a journey, giving them his uncut life story. It hurt even more, knowing that he would never see his story in book form.

How could Kalil hang himself? He seemed to be stable and content with his situation.

Maybe the closed-in walls and ills of being locked up behind jail bars took its toll on him. Maybe the guilt of leaving his baby girl to grow up without a father got to him. Maybe the death of the only woman who held his heart provoked it. The authors would never know the final chapter.

Harlem Book Fair 2007
(One Year Later)

"Fuck you! I'm glad this is our last book together." Ashley snapped her head from side to side like only a black girl can.

"Fuck me? Fuck you! Yo' solo book gon' flop anyway. You ain't shit without the kid!" JaQuavis rubbed his hand over his goatee.

"Nigga, please! My shit gon' sell, believe that. Ain't nobody gon' buy yo' corny joint. You know who the better writer is. Don't play yourself!" *This nigga really getting on my mu'fuckin' nerves,* she thought to herself.

"Yeah, sure. We'll see. I'm the better writer, and you know it. The streets gon' love my shit!"

"Yeah, the streets, and that's it," Ashley yelled. "That's all you know how to write about!"

"And the only thing you know how to write about is hustlers' wives and around-the-way girls. Yo' shit is wack! Fuck outta here!" JaQuavis waved his hand, dismissing her statement.

The very thing they were bashing each other about was the same thing that made them successful together. They told both sides of the story, which distinguished them from the other authors. Women and men could feel their work because of the unique blend that they offered their readers.

The two authors were arguing smack-dab in the middle of the 2007 Harlem Book Fair, trading insults and degrading each other's writing style, no holds barred. The disagreement had started because they couldn't agree on the direction of their next novel.

Readers and fans began to crowd around the spectacle. That's when the authors noticed that the argument was getting out of hand. They put on fake smiles, but both were boiling on the inside.

After they settled down, a crowd formed in front of their table, and immediately the two authors got back on task and began to sell and sign their own books.

Ten minutes later the crowd had left, and JaQuavis noticed a white envelope on the table in front of them that read *To Ashley & JaQuavis*. He looked around to try to figure out who left the envelope, but he had no clue. All the fans were gone, except for the last Latino woman, who Ashley was signing her book for.

Ashley pushed the book toward JaQuavis so he could sign it also, and that's when she noticed the envelope. JaQuavis signed the book and gave it to the woman before focusing his attention back on the envelope.

Exactly one year earlier someone had left them an envelope full of cash, so this envelope grabbed their full attention.

Ashley picked up the envelope and found four pieces of folded paper.

JaQuavis looked at Ashley. "What is it?"

"I don't know. Looks like a letter or something." Ashley pulled out the paper and unfolded it. In neat handwriting, the paper read: *Kalil's final chapter.*

Both of them immediately sat down and read the last chapter carefully.

Hova kneeled at the altar praying to God. He began to think about his late wife, London, and a single tear rolled down his cheek. It had been years since he'd brutally killed her, and the guilt was tugging at his heart. Even though he didn't show it while she was alive, he did love her. Every day he regretted the day that he killed her. He began to think about how he'd driven her into the arms of another man and realized that London was not being promiscuous, but just being human. She needed to feel loved.

Since the tragedy, his near-death experience had caused him to change his lifestyle and he gave his life to the Lord. He stopped going by the name Hova, reverting back to Jake. He closed his club down and left the drug game completely.

On this particular day, his conscience was eating at him. He was preparing to ask another woman for her hand in marriage. He felt he had to ask God for forgiveness one last time before popping the question. He'd found a new love and was ready to treat her like London should have been treated. He had turned over a new leaf in life and catered to her like a queen. In a sense, he was trying to find redemption. She had a beautiful child, whom he planned to treat as his own when she'd finally let the two of them meet. He had been seeing her for three months and knew that she was the new woman for him.

Later that night, he would propose to her. He wanted her to be his wife—not his trophy wife, but his wife. Jake glanced back and smiled at his love, who was sitting in the front row. He asked her to accompany him so he could settle one thing for good. Jake loved her because she was a woman of God and a faithful Christian. They bonded, not physically, but mentally. Jake had yet to make love to her, but he loved her. If she said yes, he was planning on telling her about his past, since he wanted all of the skeletons out of the closet and off his conscience.

The beauty walked behind him and began to massage his shoulders, noticing something was really bugging him. She looked down at her man's blond hair as he prayed and continued to massage his shoulders. She could tell that he was deeply in love with her. That's why what she was about to do became more difficult.

Hova unclasped his hands and reached into his pocket and pulled out a ring box. "I have to ask you something, Sunshine," he said, referring to her by the nickname he'd given her.

"What's that, Jake?" she inquired in her sweetest voice.

Jake, enjoying the massage that his woman was giving him, began to try to gather the courage to pop the question. "We've been together for three months now, and I ain't getting any younger. I want you to be mine before God. I really want to be with you for the rest of my life. Sunshine, will you be my—"

A knife swiftly sliced across Jake's throat, suddenly cutting his air supply, and blood gushed from the wound as he gripped his neck, desperately searching for air.

Destiny stepped around and let Hova see her face. She smiled at the sight of him losing his life. She opened her blouse, exposing her breasts. She wanted him to see the *RIP Kalil* tattoo she'd just gotten.

Jake read the name and the moment before he died, knew that karma had come back to bite him.

Destiny smiled and watched as his life began to slip away. "That was for Kalil," she whispered, buttoning her blouse.

She'd put on an act for three months just to get to this point. She had to do it for Kalil. She tossed the bloody knife into the pulpit and stared at the gigantic statue of Jesus that was bolted to the wall, thinking about the deceased father of her child. He had helped her in so many ways, and although she'd done him wrong, she would always love him.

Destiny left Hova's body in the church on the altar and couldn't wait to get home to her daughter Jada, now that Kalil's soul could rest in peace.